FOR
JERRY
—WHO TOOK
THE BULLET!

Thanks!

HEART
of the
Sanibel Sunset
Detective

[signature]

April  2017

Also by Ron Base

Fiction

Matinee Idol

Foreign Object

Splendido

Magic Man

The Strange

The Sanibel Sunset Detective

The Sanibel Sunset Detective Returns

Another Sanibel Sunset Detective

The Two Sanibel Sunset Detectives

The Hound of the Sanibel Sunset Detective

The Confidence Man

The Four Wives of the Sanibel Sunset Detective

The Escarpment

The Sanibel Sunset Detective Goes to London

Non-fiction

The Movies of the Eighties (with David Haslam)

If the Other Guy Isn't Jack Nicholson, I've Got the Part

Marquee Guide to Movies on Video

Cuba Portrait of an Island (with Donald Nausbaum)

www.ronbase.com

Read Ron's blog at

www.ronbase.wordpress.com

Contact Ron at

ronbase@ronbase.com

HEART

of the

Sanibel Sunset
Detective

RON BASE

West-End
Books

Library and Archives Canada Cataloguing in Publication
Base, Ron, 1948-, author
        Heart of the Sanibel sunset detective / Ron Base.
ISBN 978-0-9940645-3-0 (paperback)
        I. Title.
PS8553.A784H43 2016   C813›.54   C2016-906376-3

West-End Books
133 Mill St.
Milton, Ontario
L9T 1S1

Text design and electronic formatting: Ric Base
Cover design and coordination: Jennifer Smith
Clinton illustration and Sanibel-Captiva map: Ann Kornuta
Author photograph: Katherine Lenhoff

Woe, destruction, ruin, and decay;
The worst is death, and death will have his day.

—Richard II, Shakespeare

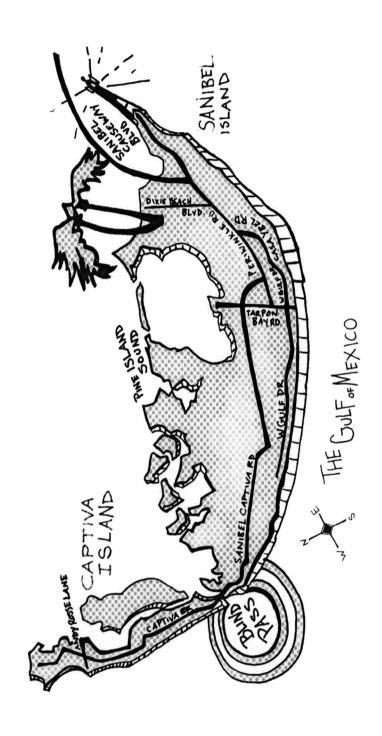

1

Tree Callister was dying.

Yes, he knew everyone was dying. He understood that. But he was actually dying. His heart was about to stop. The end was near. He was certain of it. He had known for a long time that he was closer to the finish than he was to the beginning. But now, there was no more edging toward a destination a long way off. He was there—at the end. Following a lifetime of speculation about the eventual outcome, here he was at the edge of the undiscovered country.

Tree Callister was dying.

"You're not dying," said his wife, Freddie.

"We are all dying," Tree said, repeating his latest mantra.

"Of course we are all *going* to die," Freddie agreed. "But you're not going to die today and probably not tomorrow either. Or the next day."

They were returning to Sanibel Island late in the afternoon following their annual checkup at the Cleveland Clinic, a daylong ritual that each year threw Tree into a panic as he came face to face with the notion haunting all baby boomers—that he might just be mortal.

Blood had been taken, eyes inspected, a treadmill stress test with electrodes attached to his arms and legs, and finally, a roll onto his side to allow Dr. Janet Hampshire to stick her finger up his bum.

All of which had led to one inescapable conclusion: Tree Callister was dying.

"It's not just my heart," Tree said.

"Your heart is fine," interrupted Freddie.

"They also don't like the look of my prostate. Or my kidneys."

"You're within the normal range, there's just been a slight uptick, that's all."

"Uptick," Tree gulped. "I don't like the sound of that."

"You're overreacting," said Freddie.

"They've got me scheduled to see an oncologist. If the heart doesn't get me, the cancer will. As for the kidneys I have to pee into a plastic container for twenty-four hours straight."

"Why do you have to do that?"

"So they can check my creatinine levels. They seem to be a little high. I could be on dialysis, that is if I don't have a heart attack first—or succumb to the prostate cancer that seeps into my bones."

"You're overreacting," Freddie repeated.

"You always say that."

"I only say you're overreacting when you overreact."

"It's over, I tell you. Everything is beginning to fade to black."

"I rest my case," said Freddie. "Listen, it's a beautiful, sunny day in South Florida. Nothing is fading to black."

"We're in God's waiting room down here," Tree said insistently. "They keep the lights on to reassure us old farts, just before everything goes black."

"The doctor wants you to see a couple of specialists, that's all. You feel fine don't you?"

"That's beside the point. Inside, everything is closing down."

"All of this is going to amount to nothing."

Or maybe everything, Tree thought.

"These further tests are just a precaution," Dr. Janet had said. In her white smock with her pale, smooth, unblemished skin, she was the personification of professional cool. Dr. Janet was young, there was nothing wrong with her, no disease would dare go near that perfection; she would live forever.

Tree Callister, on the other hand, was dying. All the cool, calm reassurances in the world from immortal, youthful doctors were not going to change that terrible reality. Dr. Grace Bovary, one of the clinic's psychotherapists, had tried to reassure him. "I'm a life coach," she said.

"A life coach? You help people get through life?"

She rewarded him with a fleeting smile. "Do you need help getting through life?"

"It's probably too late for me," Tree said. "I'm almost through life."

A pleasantly plump fortyish woman, Dr. Grace, too, had flawless skin. She too would live forever. She adjusted her designer glasses. "What bothers you most?" she asked.

"The fact that I have to pee into a plastic container," Tree said.

She blinked a couple of times and adjusted her glasses again. "You have to do what?"

"Pee into a plastic container," Tree said. "It's for my kidneys."

"Your kidneys?"

"There may be something wrong with them. Also my prostate and my heart."

"You have to pee into a container because of your heart?"

"No, just my kidneys," Tree advised.

"I see," Dr. Grace said in a way that suggested she didn't see at all. She peered at the computer screen.

"You're a private detective." There was a note of surprise in her voice.

"Retired," Tree said. "However, I'm considering going back to work."

Dr. Grace pulled herself away from the computer screen to give Tree a closer look. Once again she adjusted her glasses and said, "Where are you located, Tree? Where do you do business?"

"My office was on Sanibel Island. Like I said, I'm thinking of reopening it."

"You're a private detective on Sanibel Island." She tried to keep the surprise out of her voice—and failed.

"That's correct," Tree said.

"I wouldn't think there's a lot of work for a detective on Sanibel," she said slowly, choosing her words carefully.

"You would be surprised," Tree said.

"Yes, I suppose I would," Dr. Grace replied, rallying. "So, yes, I imagine detective work can produce high stress levels."

"People keep trying to kill me," Tree said.

She paused for a time before she said, "Why do you suppose people are trying to kill you, Tree?"

"There are various reasons," Tree said. "Mostly to do with the cases I've been involved in."

"And these stressful experiences…"

"I've been shot twice," Tree interjected.

Dr. Grace again tried not to look surprised—and failed. "Yes, well, as I started to say, these experiences might have something to do with producing feelings of mortality, don't you think?"

"They might," Tree said. "On the other hand I felt great when I walked in here today."

"How do you feel now?" Dr. Grace asked.

"Well, I have to pee into a plastic container, and I feel like I'm going to die," Tree said.

"I can't do much about the peeing," Dr. Grace said.

"No, I understand that may not be in the wheelhouse of a life coach," Tree said.

"But if you're feeling uneasy about death, maybe being

a private detective isn't the best occupation to pursue."

"That's been pointed out a number of times," Tree said.

"Yet here you are, thinking about going back into the work that causes you so much stress and creates these feelings of anxiety."

"Yes," Tree answered.

"Do you mind if I ask why?"

"I've discovered I get into just as much trouble when I'm not a detective as I do when I am. So I might as well be a detective."

"That doesn't make a lot of sense," Dr. Grace said.

"That seems to be the story of my life," Tree said.

"Continually doing things that don't make a lot of sense?"

Tree nodded. Dr. Grace pushed at her glasses and jotted something into the notebook open in front of her on her desk. Reading upside down, Tree could see that she wrote in small neat letters: "Afraid of peeing into a plastic container."

The life coach at work.

2

After Easter, the tourists and the aptly named snow birds fled Sanibel and its sister island Captiva, headed back north to the American Midwest where harsh winters were turning to spring and grandchildren needed attention. Sanibel emptied out at this time of the year, allowing Freddie and Tree to cross the causeway that connects the islands to the Fort Myers mainland, without waiting in traffic for an hour.

The sky as they crossed was a clear, hard blue. A lone pleasure craft threw off a silvery wake, disturbing the calm of San Carlos Bay. The local radio news was full of warnings about red tide, the high concentrations of algae that formed along the coastline turning the waters a murky red, killing fish and scaring away visitors.

Rex Baxter, Tree's long-time friend and the president of the Sanibel-Captiva Chamber of Commerce, could not tolerate the words "red" and "tide" spoken in his presence. Today, though, the water looked fine. No signs of any red tide—yet. Not that Tree was paying much attention. He was preoccupied with matters of life and death—his own life and impending death.

"There should be a week of national mourning when I'm gone," Tree said.

Freddie kept her eyes on the road, guiding her Mercedes off the causeway as she said, "I'll do my best, but we may have to settle for a day and a half of national mourning."

"Also, I will want to lie in state in the lobby of the *Sun-*

Times in Chicago so that the giants of journalism can pay their respects."

"Except the giants are all gone, and I may have a tough time finding anyone at the *Sun-Times* who even remembers when you were a reporter there."

"Also, a crypt," Tree went on.

"A crypt—a tale from the crypt," Freddie said.

"With an eternal flame burning outside to mark the enduring love the peoples of the world have for me."

"Who knew you are so loved," Freddie said. "When you got shot those two times, I wondered if anyone even liked you, let alone loved you."

"Also, please donate my papers to Yale."

"I thought you attended the School of Hard Knocks."

"I did," Tree said. "But the School of Hard Knocks doesn't accept the papers of its graduates."

"Good, because you don't have any papers."

"Are you kidding? People are still talking about my profile of Pia Zadora."

"For those of us who remember Pia Zadora," Freddie said. "Incidentally, I also have issues as a result of our visit to the clinic."

"What's wrong with you?"

"The nutritionist thinks I should eat more almonds."

"That's it?"

"That's quite enough, don't you think?"

"I knew it," Tree said. "You're going to live forever."

"Someone has to stay behind," Freddie said. "I'll wear black, wail at the crypt, and make sure the eternal flame doesn't go out."

"I appreciate that," Tree said.

"It's the least I can do," Freddie said.

Yes, Tree mused, Freddie would be fine. He glanced at that proud, lovely profile, green eyes straight ahead, concentrating on the road, the blond hair that recently had reached her shoulders framing that ageless face he had fallen for the moment they met at that Chicago dinner party, so long ago now he could hardly remember a life before Freddie—or chose not to remember his life before Freddie. Yes, best not to think too much about that messy part of his journey.

She had been a successful supermarket executive; he was the wild and crazy newspaper reporter no woman in her right mind should have become involved with. Well, maybe not that wild and not as crazy by the time he met her, but he wasn't exactly prime marriage material, that was for sure.

No sooner had they started dating than Tree suffered chest pains while visiting Chicago's WBBM-TV where his pal Rex Baxter was the popular weatherman. He had been rushed to emergency, everyone convinced—Tree included—that he'd had a heart attack. Fortunately, it turned out to be a false alarm. The only good part of the whole episode was Freddie who had brought flowers when she visited him.

Tree knew right then and there that somehow, some way, he was going to marry this spectacular woman.

And he did just that, although Freddie did wonder aloud how it was she managed to marry a guy with a name like Tree.

The last thing either of them expected was Sanibel Island, but Tree had been downsized, as they chose to call it, from the *Sun-Times*, throwing his professional life into a tailspin.

Freddie, meanwhile, had tired of the rat race that was Chicago retailing. Offered a job running a small chain of supermarkets along the west coast of Florida, she surprised everyone, including herself, by accepting it.

The next thing, they were moving to the island where Tree had vacationed as a child. Eventually, Freddie headed a syndicate of investors that bought out the supermarket chain. Not long after that, she was forced out by the very investors she had brought together in the first place.

Now she was a woman of leisure, she said. It was a time for exploration and taking time before deciding what to do next.

Tree's cellphone vibrated in his pocket. He fished it out and looked at the screen, not recognizing the number. He swiped open the phone. A voice said, "Tree Callister. It's Dan Meade."

"Dandy Dan? The football player? From high school?"

"None other, buddy." Dandy Dan's voice was a cheerful rasp in Tree's ear. "It's been awhile."

"Try fifty years," Tree said.

"Time flies, buddy. What can I tell you?"

"Tell me how you're doing."

"Well, buddy, that's why I'm calling," Dandy Dan said cheerfully. "You see, I'm dying."

Isn't everyone? Tree thought. Isn't everyone?

3

There's a big plastic container on your desk," Rex Baxter said the next morning when he brought coffee into Tree's reconstituted office on the second floor of the Sanibel-Captiva Chamber of Commerce Visitors Center. "What? Did you run out of gas?"

"I have to pee into it," Tree said.

"You're kidding," Rex said.

"For twenty-four hours," Tree added.

"Why would you have to do that?"

"For my kidneys."

"There's something wrong with your kidneys?"

"There could be, yeah."

"And you have to fill that thing up before they can ascertain that?"

"Apparently."

"Don't tell me you brought a plastic container full of pee into this office." Rex sounded shocked.

"Of course not," Tree said. "What do you take me for?"

"These days, anything is possible," Rex said.

"Besides, you keep it in a refrigerator."

"You keep a plastic tub full of piss in your fridge?"

"Doesn't everybody?"

"When are you supposed to do this?"

"As soon as I can," Tree said. "The thing is, I haven't started yet. I guess I should. I'm trying to get up the nerve to do it."

"Why not go home and do it today?"

"Because I have to meet Dan Meade."

"Dan Meade? The football player? Dandy Dan Meade?"

"That's the one."

"You mean to tell me you know Dandy Dan Meade?"

"I'm not sure I know him since I haven't seen him for fifty years, but we went to high school together," Tree said.

"You never said anything," Rex said.

"Never crossed my mind," Tree said.

"Four seasons with the Chicago Bears, maybe the best all-round running back who ever played for the team. I would have thought you'd say something."

"It's not like we were close buddies or anything. I guess we hung out for a while in high school, but he was into that whole jock thing, and I wasn't."

"Well, I'm a football fan, and I loved Dandy Dan Meade. He was young and glamorous and fun at a time in football when there were not a lot of fun, glamorous guys around. I never understood why he left when he did."

"I'll ask him when I see him," Tree said.

"You're kidding." Rex looked even more astonished. "You're actually meeting Dandy Dan. He's here? On the island?"

"Looks like it. He's sending a car for me this afternoon."

"What's he want?"

"No idea," Tree said. "He said he found out I was on the island and wants to get together."

"You do know he's now this *über* rich guy. Got into online sports betting early. Made a fortune."

"But he's retired now," Tree said.

"So he says."

"What's that mean?"

"According to the *New York Times*, he might not be as retired as he says he is. The suggestion is that he says he's out of online gambling so the feds will leave him alone. But the feds aren't buying his retirement."

"We'll see," Tree said.

"Could be a case," Rex said.

"I doubt that."

"Why not? The Sanibel Sunset Detective Agency is back in business, is it not?"

"I'm not so sure it is," Tree said.

"What do you mean? You're sitting here in your office, aren't you? You're open for business."

"I'm sitting here in an empty office in the Chamber," Tree amended. "I'm not sure it's any more than that."

"What's Freddie think of you being back here?"

"She thinks I need a distraction."

"From what?"

"From thinking I'm going to die."

"I've got bad news for you," Rex said. "We're all going to die."

"I understand that," Tree said.

"What? You thought you could get a pass?"

"We were at the Cleveland Clinic the other day." He pointed to the plastic container on his desk. "That's why I've got this."

"If it's any consolation, I've got heart bypass surgery to look forward to." Rex sipped at his coffee.

"You keep putting it off," Tree said. "You're worse than I am. I think about death all the time. You keep ignoring it."

"Not me," Rex said. "I don't know what you're talking about."

He rose to his feet. "While I'm still alive, I'd better get to work and earn my keep." He started toward the door, then stopped and turned. "Let's end this on an optimistic note."

"What's that?"

"All your life, you've never had a pot to piss in." Rex pointed a finger at the container. "Now you've got one."

———

After Rex departed, Tree sat staring at the framed wall photograph of the young woman in a bikini catching a swordfish. The photograph was somewhat faded now. The young woman had been catching that swordfish ever since he occupied the office.

For the time being, he was more or less back to where he had started in the private detective business, his attempt to find a life for himself after being downsized at the *Sun-Times*, ending the newspaper life he thought would go on forever. He had discovered time and again over the past few years, nothing goes on forever. Not life. Certainly not newspapers.

So here he was a detective again. Or was he? Was he ever a detective? Well, not much of one, that was certain. Stumbling along, deluding himself, he supposed, as he made his irrevocable way toward the abyss.

The sound of footsteps coming up the stairs drew him out of his reverie. A large shape filled the entrance to the office. The shape took the form of an African-American man in a dark blue suit, the shaved sides of his head topped by a nest of artfully arranged dreadlocks. A mustache trailed to a neatly clipped goatee framing a gleaming smile. "Mr. Tree?" a deep, rumbling voice asked.

"Yes," Tree said.

"I am Kobus, man. I've come to take you to Mr. Dan."

4

Tree wasn't sure what he would find after he followed Kobus into the parking lot, but he wasn't expecting the little red pickup truck. "Mr. Dan does not like a fuss," Kobus said.

"I didn't know Mr. Dan lives on the island," Tree said as he seated himself inside the cramped interior of the truck.

"Mr. Dan does not live on this island," Kobus said.

"He doesn't? Then where is he?"

Kobus didn't answer. He concentrated on turning the key in the ignition. The truck growled, sputtered, and died. Kobus tried again—and again. Finally, after a couple of more attempts, the engine coughed to life, and Kobus started out of the parking lot.

"If Dan isn't here, where is he?" Tree asked.

"Not to worry, man," Kobus said. "We're not going far."

"All right. I won't worry. Have you worked a long time for Dan?"

"Mr. Dan does not like me giving out personal information," Kobus said.

"I see," Tree said.

"Me? I like to talk," Kobus said cheerfully. "All the time I'm growing up in Stellenbosch, my mom say to me, 'Kobus, you shouldn't talk so much. You will get yourself in nothing but trouble.'"

"So, did it get you into trouble?"

Kobus presented him with a dazzling smile. "Got me out of Stellenbosch, that's for sure."

"You're from South Africa."

"You see? I talk too much. Mr. Dan does not like that." Kobus opened another wide smile as he guided the truck across the causeway.

"But I will tell you this much," Kobus continued. "My mom was wrong. I talk and talk and my mouth took me around the world to Mr. Dan and the good life here in America."

Thirty minutes later, Kobus turned the little truck onto Captain Channing Page Drive and Tree realized they were headed for Page Field, the old Fort Myers air terminal that had been replaced in 1983 by the larger Southwest Florida International Airport. Nowadays, Page Field mostly catered to private aircraft.

Kobus parked adjacent to a sleek white tube of a jet at the edge of the tarmac. "What is this?" Tree demanded.

Kobus turned off the ignition. "A Cessna CJ3. Mr. Dan's private jet."

"I need to know where you are taking me," Tree said.

"Man, you are asking the wrong person for such information," Kobus said. He opened the driver's-side door. "Come along, and you will receive all the answers you require."

Tree got out of the truck as a tall, athletic-looking woman in a white pantsuit came down the steps from the jet. "There you are, Mr. Callister. Just in time. We are about to take off."

The woman spoke in precisely modulated, British-accented tones. A long, narrow face was framed by smartly cut chestnut hair. She punctuated her words with a firm handshake.

"I must tell you, I am not in favor of this."

"I'm sorry," Tree said, squinting to get a better look at her. "What is it you're not in favor of?"

"Dan is not well. We are trying to care for him, but he's stubborn and won't listen to anyone when he doesn't feel like it."

"I don't know who you are."

The tall woman took her hand away, appearing surprised. "Who am I?"

"You see," Kobus announced with glee. "I told you he would ask many questions."

The tall woman frowned. "That's quite enough, Kobus." She gave Tree a look and said, "Yes, I suppose I'd better tell you who I am. Prudence Colt. Everyone calls me Pru. I work for Dan. He sent me along to make sure you are comfortable on the flight, which I will do, of course, even though I do believe this trip is unnecessary and will only further jeopardize my employer's already fragile health."

"Flight? Flight to where?"

"I'm not at liberty to give you that information at this time, Mr. Callister."

"You're not at liberty to tell me where you are taking me?"

"It's like I told you, man." More glee in Kobus's voice. "Mr. Dan does not like too much talk."

"Kobus, I said that's enough," Pru snapped. She addressed Tree in the same voice his middle-school math teacher had used to give him a detention. "Mr. Callister, you have agreed to meet with Dan on a business-related matter. This is how he does business. You are completely safe, if that's what's worrying you."

"What's wrong with Dan that you're so concerned about him?"

"This is information you will have to get from Dan.

I'm not at liberty to say. Are you coming with us or not, Mr. Callister?"

"It doesn't look as though I have much choice, does it?"

"You can choose not to go," Pru said. "You have that choice."

Tree thought about it and then shrugged. "All right. Let's get this over with."

"Come along then. We don't have a lot of time to waste." She turned and started back for the plane.

Tree looked at Kobus who shrugged and smiled. "She's just like my grandmother back in Stellenbosch. A real monster, that woman."

"Your grandmother or Ms. Colt?" inquired Tree.

Kobus just smiled.

———

The beige and ivory interior of the Cessna was cramped but comfortable. Tree watched out the window as Fort Myers and the Gulf of Mexico grew smaller and then were lost in a blast of sunlight.

Tree sat back and closed his eyes. Yes, that was better. Somehow, up here, preoccupied with where he was going and what would happen when he got there, death seemed distant, something he left behind in Fort Myers.

Over the drone of the engines, Tree heard Prudence Colt say, "Kobus, ask Mr. Callister if he would like something to drink."

"You ask him," Kobus retorted. "I am not a servant."

"You are what I say you are—and right now you're an employee asking Mr. Callister if he would like something to drink."

"I would rather know where we are headed," Tree said, opening his eyes.

"See? He doesn't want anything. I know this man; he is not troublesome, like some others."

From her seat facing Tree, Pru Colt made a face and said, "What about it, Mr. Callister? Can we get you something to drink?"

"No, I don't want anything," Tree said.

"See?" Kobus said. "Now you have upset Mr. Tree."

"Are you upset, Mr. Tree?" Pru asked.

"How much longer is this going to take?"

Pru glanced at her watch. "Won't be long now."

Tree pulled his phone out of his pocket. Pru immediately sat up, looking alarmed. "What are you doing?"

"What does it look like? I'm making a phone call."

"To whom are you making this call?" Pru made it sound as if she had caught him stealing her expensive watch.

"Sorry, Mr. Tree," Kobus said with a laugh, "no signal up here."

"Besides, we would prefer you not make any phone calls until after you have talked to Dan." Pru's voice was carefully modulated, as though determined to remain calm.

"You're kidding. You mean to tell me I can't make a phone call?"

Pru forced a smile. "It's like Kobus says. There is no signal available, anyway."

Kobus peered out the window. The smile lit his face as he announced, "Here we are."

The Cessna had dipped over a city nestled against a river bisected by a gleaming white suspension bridge. Pru made another face as she addressed Tree. "Better fasten your seatbelt, Mr. Callister. We are about to land in Savannah."

5

Tree waited with Pru Colt outside on the arrivals level at Savannah/Hilton Head International Airport while Kobus went off. A few minutes later he reappeared behind the wheel of a white Lincoln. Pru slipped into the front beside Kobus, directing Tree to sit in the back.

"Is Dan in Savannah?" he asked as Kobus pulled the Lincoln away from the airport.

Neither of them answered.

They drove into town along West Bay Street. Kobus turned the Lincoln onto Jefferson and pulled over at the corner. Pru turned to Tree and said, "He's over by the Johnny Mercer statue."

"The Johnny Mercer statue?"

"You'll see. At the edge of Ellis Square. I must warn you, Mr. Callister."

"Warn me about what?"

"He is not himself."

"None of us is," Tree said.

"I remind you, Mr. Callister, that I objected strenuously to this meeting."

"Thanks for the reminder," Tree said.

"Get out, Mr. Callister. The journey is over."

Tree could see Kobus behind the wheel. He didn't turn, but part of his wry smile was visible as he shook his head back and forth.

The light was fading across what was less a square and more a large circular space fronting a pedestrian walkway flanked by shops and restaurants. At the end of the walkway Tree could see the outline of a bronze statue. Nearby, a man wearing a baseball cap, dressed in a navy blue pullover, faded jeans, and worn sneakers, sat on a bench reading a newspaper. Tree started toward him.

At this time of the evening, few pedestrians were around. As Tree approached, he could see that the bronze figure wore a fedora and leaned rather incongruously against a fire hydrant. He, too, was reading a newspaper.

The figure not made of bronze saw Tree and set his newspaper aside. He gave a vacant look and said, "Forgive me for not standing. It's easier if I don't stand."

"Sure, I understand," Tree said.

Dandy Dan Meade was no longer so dandy, far removed from the handsome, All-American face Tree remembered from high school. Age had made him pale and haggard-looking, a ghost of his former self. Or maybe we are all ghosts, Tree thought as he pasted on a smile and decided he should identify himself. "Dan, it's Tree Callister."

A light flared in Dan's dull eyes beneath the peak of the baseball cap. He worked up a smile as he took Tree's hand. "Of course, yes," he said in a raspy voice. "I asked them to bring you here, didn't I?"

"I'm not sure why exactly, but yes, you did," Tree said. "How have you been?"

"I've had some health issues, Tree, but I'm still here. That's what counts, isn't it? We're both still here."

"That's right, Dan," Tree said.

"So every night, I come over here and talk to my friend, Johnny." He nodded his head toward the bronze statue.

"So that's Johnny Mercer," Tree said, the recognition dawning. "The guy who wrote the lyrics for 'Moon River.'"

"And for 'Charade' as well."

"The theme song from the Cary Grant-Audrey Hepburn movie," Tree said.

"That's right, although, unfortunately, the movie barely makes use of it. One of the great unrecognized pop songs. A kind of bittersweet perfection to it. You can't imagine the creative genius required from Johnny and the composer Henry Mancini to produce something so entirely original and yet so simple."

"Yes, it's a wonderful song," Tree said.

"Johnny is a native of Savannah," Dan went on. "His house on Bull Street where he grew up is something of a historical landmark. I come over here in the evenings and I sit with Johnny, and I feel at peace with the world. Join me, please, and let's talk. It's been a long time, and so much has happened to both of us."

Tree settled beside Dan on the bench. The twilight glinted off the Johnny Mercer statue, throwing a golden glow over Ellis Square. Dan took a deep breath as though inhaling his surroundings. "So nice at this time of night," he said. "My mind seems clearer when I'm here with Johnny, less foggy." He became silent as though reflecting on his state of mind. Then he looked at Tree and said, "You know what I aim to do, Tree? Just between the two of us?"

"What's that, Dan?"

"I love Johnny Mercer's house. I'm going to buy it. As soon as I can, I'm going to buy it and live in it. How do you like that?"

Tree wasn't certain how to respond, so he simply squeezed Dan's arm. "It's good to see you again after all this time."

"High school buddies, eh, Tree? Who knew where we would end up all these years later?"

"Well, I think we all knew you'd play football, Dan. And I suppose I knew I would get into the newspaper business. But you're right. No one could have predicted we'd end up old men at dusk sitting in a square in Savannah with Johnny Mercer."

"You're my huckleberry friend, Tree," Dan said. "You really are."

Tree wasn't so sure about that, but he said, "That's very sweet." If Dan wanted to remember their childhood acquaintance as enduring friendship, who was he to argue?

"And now you're out of the newspaper business," Dan said.

"How do you know?" Tree asked.

Dan delivered a secretive smile. "I did some poking around, Tree, after I saw a story about you in one of the Chicago newspapers. A private detective on Sanibel Island, something of a local hero it turns out."

"Not much of a hero, I'm afraid."

"Losing your job at the *Sun-Times*, that must have been painful."

"Yes, it was," Tree said. "A life's work, part of your identity—my entire identity if I'm being honest—and suddenly it's all gone. Not a lot of fun."

"But you can't go on being a football player forever, and I guess you can't go on being a newspaperman, either. We've both had to change, adapt to the realities of life."

"Yes, I guess you're right, Dan."

"So now you've got a new identity."

"Yeah, well, I do wonder," Tree said. "I'm not sure how much of a detective I am. I retired for a while."

"But now you're back to work?"

"I suppose so. According to my wife, Freddie, I never really retired in the first place."

"I am so glad to hear that, Tree. You see there is more than simple nostalgia for an old and valued friendship that brings us back together."

"I have to admit I was surprised when I heard from you," Tree said.

"I need your help, old friend."

"Okay," Tree said slowly. "But I'm not sure if I can be of much help."

"You are the only person who can. I'm totally relying on you."

"I'm not sure what to say, Dan."

"You don't have to say anything. Just listen to what I have to tell you."

"I'll be glad to do that," Tree said.

6

As though to settle in for his story, Dan removed his baseball cap. Beneath the cap he was almost bald. "I should tell you, Tree," he said, "I'm suffering from chronic traumatic encephalopathy, otherwise known as CTE. You know what that is?"

"A form of dementia, isn't it? It's common among football players who have received frequent blows to the head, concussions."

"That's right. It's a progressive degenerative disease. I've obviously been suffering from it for some time, but lately it's gotten worse. I'm losing my memory, Tree. Everything is slipping away from me."

"I'm so sorry to hear this, Dan."

"To make matters worse, I'm being investigated by federal authorities."

"Investigated? For what?" Tree already knew about the investigation, but he wanted to hear it from Dan.

"As you may know, after I left the Bears, I got involved in a couple of gambling things in Las Vegas and Atlantic City. Investments mostly, no big deal. But then a few years ago, I invested in a fledgling offshore gaming company, run by a guy named Sonny Picas. He'd started out with telephones but now he was going to computers and needed start-up capital. Computers? I thought. Who uses computers to bet? What did I know? But I liked Sonny; he was a young guy who talked a good game. So I took a chance and invested a few hundred thousand. Next thing, Sonny's business takes off and instead of being a fairly wealthy football player, I am now worth hundreds of millions, and it happened practically overnight."

"I read something about this," Tree said. "But Internet sports betting is now illegal, is it not?"

"I guess it depends on your definition of illegal. It wasn't illegal until 2006 when Congress passed legislation prohibiting the use of credit cards for online gambling, which essentially outlawed the industry. That was enough for me. I sold my interests back to Sonny and got out. By that time I knew I was in trouble with my health and just didn't want any more hassles. But that didn't satisfy the Justice Department, apparently. Their investigators still think I'm involved."

"But you're not, is that correct?"

Dan hesitated before he said, "Yes, that's correct." He paused again. "However, like I told you, I'm having memory problems. Increasingly, there are large parts of my life I can't remember. For instance, I know I played for the Chicago Bears, but only because people keep telling me I did. I can't remember a thing about that period. It's like a bottomless black hole that someone poured my memory into."

"Yet you remembered me," Tree said.

"Curious, isn't it? What you remember and what gets lost down that black hole. For instance..." He fished into his pocket and brought out a sheet of paper.

He handed it to Tree. "This has me very worried."

Tree looked at it. The single sheet contained three names and addresses, hand-printed.

"I don't understand," Tree said. "This is just a list of names."

"But who are these people and why did I make the list?"

"This is your handwriting?"

Harry Panama
210 East Libery St.
Savannah, GA.

Will Mickens
111 Cholokka Blvd.
Micanopy, Fl.

A.T. Kamala
24 Massachusetts Ave.
Washington, D.C.

"As far as I know, it is."

"There are three names," Tree said. "None of the three means anything to you?"

"Nothing."

"Can't you ask someone? The people who work for you?"

"That's just it. With the feds investigating me, I don't want anyone to know. I feel I can't trust anyone right now."

"Not Prudence Colt? Or Kobus?"

"They are plotting against me," he said.

"Come on, Dan. Do you really believe that?"

"Ex-wives, too." There was agitated certainty in his voice. "All sorts of madness is unfolding as we speak. Saudis. There are Saudis involved."

"Saudis?"

"And Russians."

"Okay."

"It's a mess," Dan said. "You are the only person I can trust."

"Me?" Tree looked at him in astonishment.

"You are the one person I know who will work for my best interests and keep everything confidential."

"That's good of you to say that. But I have to tell you, what you're thinking about me, it's not really based on anything."

Dan looked suddenly hurt and vulnerable. "What are you saying? I can't trust you?"

"Yes, of course you can."

"There you go. My faith is not misplaced."

"I'm not sure what you want me to do, Dan."

"I need you to find out who these three people are and why they are on the list," Dan said. "I need you to do this as quickly as possible."

"How much trouble do you think you're in?"

"I don't know. I'll know better once I understand more about this list and the people on it."

Tree looked at the list. "Washington makes sense, I suppose, so does Savannah. But who do you know in Micanopy, Florida?"

Dan shook his head. "I don't even know where it is, do you?"

"Never heard of it," Tree said.

Dan reached into his inside pocket again and this time withdrew a slim white business envelope. He handed it to Tree. "This is a cashier's check for twenty-five thousand dollars."

"That's far too much, Dan."

"No it isn't, Tree. If you can help me out, it's not too much at all."

"I'm not sure what to say."

"Say you'll help me, Tree. You are my only hope."

"Dan, I can't possibly be your only hope."

He didn't answer. Tree saw that he was staring off, his eyes growing wild. "They're coming!" he announced, and plucked the list from Tree's fingers. "They must not see this. They must not!"

He struggled up and limped over to the Johnny Mercer statue and slipped the list out of sight beneath the newspaper Johnny was reading.

A moment later, Pru Colt strode into view, followed by a lingering Kobus. "Dan, it's time to go," she brusquely announced.

"Tree and I were just getting caught up," Dan said in a surprisingly meek voice.

"It's time for your medication and you haven't eaten anything," Pru said.

"Give us a few more minutes," Dan said, a pleading note in his voice.

"Dan. Please. Let's not argue."

Dan turned to Tree and shrugged helplessly. "What can you do? Duty calls."

"Are you all right, Dan?"

Pru stepped forward so that she was between the two men. "He's doing just fine, Mr. Callister. Now Kobus will drive you to the airport for the flight back to Fort Myers."

Tree addressed Dan. "Is that okay with you?"

"Yes, of course. I was supposed to fly as well, but I've decided against it. Pru says I'm too tired to travel."

"That's right, Dan, you are," Pru said.

He forced a smile onto his pale, haggard face. "It's good to see you, old friend."

"We will be in touch," Tree said.

"Yes, we will," Dan said.

Tree reached down and picked up Dan's discarded baseball cap. He saw that his name and an address were stitched inside: Daniel Meade, 51 Drayton St., Savannah, GA.

"Don't forget your hat," Tree said, handing it to Dan.

The old man placed it on his head. He held out his hand. Tree took it and then embraced him. Dan whispered into his ear, "You *are* my only hope."

7

It was nearly dark as Kobus drove the Lincoln toward the airport. He was unusually quiet. Tree kept thinking about the list hidden in the folds of Johnny Mercer's newspaper in Ellis Square, and how he was going to get back there to pick it up.

Kobus shook his head and looked concerned, "I thought Mr. Dan was coming with us."

"Pru said he wasn't well enough to travel."

"Does not make any sense," Kobus said. "All he has to do is sit on a comfortable plane. I do not understand it. Why would she keep him in Savannah?"

"Where was Dan supposed to go?"

The question was met with silence. After a few minutes, Tree said, "Sad about Dan. I hated to see him like that."

"Football really messed him up," Kobus replied.

"How long have you been with him?"

Kobus cast Tree a sly glance, then returned his eyes to the roadway, and smiled. "Mr. Dan would not like that. Neither would the Wicked Bitch."

"Is that what you call Prudence Colt?"

"What would you call her, man? I mean, she is *bad*. I've been with Mr. Dan for five years now, and I have seen plenty of crap go down. But that Wicked Bitch, she's been with him *forever*, man."

"But they're not married."

"You kidding me, man? Who would marry her? The way I hear it, she was the secretary to Mr. Dan's wife, Doris, and after she left him, the Wicked Bitch just stayed on—even after he got married again."

"Dan's remarried?"

Kobus shrugged and was silent. Tree said, "Sounds like he's not married now."

"But the Wicked Bitch is still around. Clinging to Mr. Dan like a parasite."

"But he obviously needs help," Tree said.

"Sure does. He's getting worse, no doubt about that. But he does not need to be a *prisoner.*"

"Is that what he is?"

"What would you call it, man? She says she's protecting him, and maybe there's some truth to that. Some pretty strange things happening around here, let me tell you. I mean biggest surprise ever is you turning up today. I never would have thought she'd let it happen." He cast Tree another sly look. "What was all that about back there, anyway?"

"Two high school buddies getting together, shooting the breeze, that's all," Tree said carefully.

"Shooting the breeze? How do you shoot the breeze?"

"It's a figure of speech," Tree said.

"Well, okay, but something goes down, I think maybe you're part of it. Just so you know."

"What do you think is going down, Kobus?"

"Don't know. But like I said, strange things are happening. Mr. Dan, he used to be involved in some pretty shady stuff, I hear. Some bad dudes show up from time to time."

"Russians?"

Kobus threw Tree a glance and shrugged. "Some sort of foreign fellas. Don't know where they come from exactly. Nicely dressed. But with stone faces. Like they couldn't care if you lived or you died."

"What do they want with Dan?"

Another shrug; another quick glance in Tree's direction. "Mr. Dan says he's out of the gambling business. But these foreign fellas, they are not out of it. So you have to wonder."

"I hear what you're saying," Tree said. "But we knew each other in high school. That's the extent of it. Nothing to do with gambling."

More or less true, Tree thought as Kobus turned into the airport. He was still trying to come up with the excuse that would allow him to go back to Ellis Square for that list.

Through a chain-link fence, Tree could see the Cessna gleaming beneath lights. Kobus parked the Lincoln at the edge of the tarmac. "Okay," he said, "here we are."

Tree got out, his mind whirling, trying to figure a way to avoid getting on that jet.

He faced Kobus coming around the front of the car. "Let's go back," he said.

Kobus appeared surprised. "Go back? Why do you want to go back?"

"You said Dan was supposed to get on the plane," Tree said. "You're worried about him. I can tell that. Let's go back to Savannah and make sure he's all right."

"Too late for that." Kobus looked nervous.

"It's not too late. How can it be too late?"

"Get on the plane, Mr. Tree. We have to go."

"I want to make sure Dan's all right. You drive me back there, Kobus."

Tree started back into the Lincoln.

"Mr. Tree!"

Tree looked up to see Kobus with his arm outstretched. There was a gun in his hand. Pointed at Tree.

"You just stop right there." Kobus, his face hard, spoke

in a surprisingly authoritative voice. The nice guy had disappeared.

"What are you doing, Kobus?" Tree said.

"Come along to the plane, man. Don't mess with me, okay? I want you to board the plane."

Before Tree had a chance to argue further, the side of the Cessna appeared to open up, like a jagged angry mouth spitting flames. This was followed an instant later by a loud boom and a rush of hot air. Black smoke shot high into the night sky along with pieces of metal from the plane's fuselage.

Tree found himself momentarily airborne, the force of the explosion throwing him into the fence.

His ears ringing, Tree struggled to his feet. Smoldering debris littered the tarmac. The miracle was that none of it had hit him. Then he saw why. The Lincoln had served as a shield from the blast. The side of the car facing the plane was dented and scorched.

Kobus had not been so lucky. Tree found him beside the Lincoln. Debris from the explosion had nearly ripped his head off and torn a gaping hole in his back. Flames danced along his pant leg. Tree called his name and looked around desperately for something to extinguish the flames. There was nothing.

There was no sign of the gun Kobus had been holding, but not far from his dead extended hand, something gleamed on the tarmac.

The key for the Lincoln.

Tree bent and scooped it up. He stood there, trying to clear the buzzing in his ears, coming to terms with the fact that someone had just blown up Dandy Dan Meade's plane and almost killed Tree. Dan Meade was supposed to be on that plane.

Except he wasn't.

Tree thought of the list Dan gave him.

Then he thought that whoever did this, having missed Dan at the airport, might try again. He had to warn Dan before it was too late.

The passenger-side windows of the Lincoln were blown out. The hood had buckled and there was a crack in the windshield. Tree went around to the driver's side. He wrenched the door open and got behind the wheel. To his relief, the Lincoln started up.

He put it in drive and started forward away from the burning plane. As he swung into the street, he could hear the wail of approaching sirens.

A sound he had heard too many times before.

8

The Lincoln's engine made curious sounds as Tree picked up speed through darkened Savannah streets. The dashboard GPS said he was twenty-four minutes from 51 Drayton Street. When he turned onto Liberty, the Lincoln began making loud clanging sounds. Tree pulled over to the curb and turned off the ignition.

He got out of the car and started along the street. He went through a park, the moss hanging in long streams from the oak trees on either side of the pathway, backlit by coach lamps. A Revolutionary War hero he couldn't identify glared down at him, and Tree half expected him to demand, "Who goes there?"

Who indeed.

He found number 51 on the far side of the park, one of those lovely old Savannah homes you see in the tourist photos, red brick with bowed windows, artfully framed by a cast-iron fence, and lots more hanging moss. Tree went up the steps and rang the bell. No one answered. After a couple of minutes, he rang again. The drapes were pulled over the windows, but he could see a light behind them. Surely, given his state, Dan Meade would not have been left alone. He pounded on the door.

Finally, he tried the latch. As it had on too many similar occasions, the door opened. Tree's heart was abruptly in his throat. This was frighteningly familiar, he thought. He pushed the door open further and stepped inside.

An entrance hall, a ceiling reaching for the stars, and a winding staircase capable of transporting you to those stars. Delicately shaded lamps lining a sideboard produced a subtle golden light. Music came from somewhere deep in the house: Hoagy Carmichael singing his own composition, "Lazy Bones," with lyrics by the great Johnny Mercer.

Tree moved across the hall into a sitting room the size of a basketball court. Hoagy's laconic drawl accused Tree of being a lazy bones… "A-sleepin' all the day."

He wished.

The sitting room was decorated with the solid, comfortable furniture Hoagy and Johnny might have sat on at the end of a day composing great songs together. The music had grown louder. "You'll never earn a dime that way," Hoagy advised, before adding that the lazy bones to whom the song was addressed never heard a word he had to say.

Prudence Colt might have been listening to Hoagy singing Johnny's lyrics, but she wasn't listening any longer. Instead, she lay on her back staring wide-eyed at the high ceiling, mouth open as though she had been trying to call out before someone plunged a kitchen knife into her chest with such force the blade had gone in almost to the hilt.

Tree knew better than to touch the body—to touch anything if he ever wanted to get out of the mess he had once again stumbled into. Further, if Kobus was dead and now Prudence Colt, that didn't bode well for Dan Meade. There was no sign of him on the main floor. He wasn't upstairs, either.

By the time Tree returned to the entrance hall, Hoagy had stopped singing about lazy bones. Tree took a deep breath, opened the door and stepped outside. The sound of crickets and distant traffic greeted him. Lamplight from the adjacent square seeped through the live oaks hinting at gothic mystery, ghosts slipping through wispy shadows.

Tree retraced his path into the park without encountering anyone and, he hoped, not being seen. Somehow, he stumbled his way along shadowed streets until, more by accident than any sense of where he was going, he stepped into a brightly lit pedestrian thoroughfare. People sauntered along, listening to a street musician with a wailing saxophone, avoiding the young man hawking city ghost tours. Plenty of ghosts out tonight, Tree thought, and some of them might be trying to kill him.

Johnny Mercer grinned as Tree approached. It was the smile that would always light Johnny's world, holding open the newspaper he would never close. The list was right where Dan had hidden it. He plucked the single sheet out of the fold in Johnny's newspaper and silently thanked him.

Tree walked across the square to a bench and slumped onto it, allowing exhaustion to wash over him. He wanted to curl up on the bench, close his eyes, and sleep. Instead, he pulled out his cellphone. Freddie answered almost as soon as he finished punching out her number. "Where are you?" she demanded.

"Don't get mad at me," Tree said.

"I'm going to kill you," Freddie said.

"I think someone's already trying to do that," Tree said.

"Tree, what's going on? What have you got yourself into?" There was anguish in Freddie's voice.

"I'm not sure, but none of it's good. Right now, I need you to come and get me."

"Where are you?"

"Savannah."

There was a long pause before Freddie said, "How did you manage to end up in Savannah?"

"It's a long story," Tree said.

"It always is," Freddie said.

"I'll tell you all about it when you get here," Tree said. "Right now, I need you to go online and get me the name of a hotel where I can hole up. I'm in Ellis Square in downtown Savannah. Can you find something nearby for me?"

"Hold on," Freddie said. A moment later she was back on the line. "There is the Cotton Sail Hotel. It's a short walk from where you are, on the waterfront, and they've got vacancies."

"I'll check in and wait for you," Tree said.

"Are you all right?"

"I'll be better once you're here," Tree said.

"Listen, there's something else I have to tell you," Freddie said. "I don't want you getting upset."

"Okay," Tree said.

"Rex collapsed late this afternoon."

Tree felt his stomach twist into a knot. "Collapsed?"

"He's all right for now, resting at Lee Memorial Health Center. You know he's supposed to have had heart bypass surgery."

"He keeps putting it off."

"Now he's going to have the surgery whether he likes it or not."

"I'll call him when we're off the line," Tree said.

"Okay. I'm on my way."

"Thank you, my love," Tree said.

"Just be very careful," Freddie said. "Get to the Cotton Sail and stay in your room until I get there."

"I love you," Tree said.

Freddie hung up without replying, never a good sign, Tree thought.

––––––––––

Rex came on the line and said in a weak voice, "Don't even think about giving me hell."

"As long as you're not dead," Tree said.

"Are you kidding? It's going to take more than a little heart attack to kill me. Where are you, anyway?"

"I'm in Savannah."

"Savannah? How much trouble are you in?"

"What makes you think I'm in trouble?"

"It's Tuesday. You're in trouble."

"It's not Tuesday, I'm not in trouble, but I should be there with you."

"All this time you're worried about dying, and I'm the one on death's door."

"What are they telling you?"

"Lies, all lies," Rex said. "But just in case, I'm scheduled for surgery first thing in the morning. By the time you get back I'll be fit as a fiddle and ready for love."

"I'm worried about you."

"Don't worry about me. Worry about yourself."

"I'm all right."

"Quit lying to me," Rex said.

"I don't want anything to happen to you."

"Of course you don't. If anything happens, you'll have to start paying rent."

"I won't have anyone to get me out of the trouble I get myself into."

Rex said, "What kind of trouble are you in?"

"What makes you think I'm in trouble?"

"Like I said, it's Tuesday, you're in trouble."

"And like I said, it's not Tuesday. Just get better."

"What's politically correct these days?" Rex said. "Is it okay for two men to say they love each other?"

"I believe it is," Tree said.

"Then I love you, old pal."

Tree choked and said, "You're my oldest friend in the world."

"Does that mean you love me?"

"Of course it does."

"Then I can survive anything," Rex said.

9

Tree's room at the Cotton Sail featured a view of the docks and the Savannah River, although tonight Tree wasn't paying much attention to views. He stripped off his clothes and took a long shower. Feeling somewhat better, he came back into the room, wrapping himself in the hotel-supplied robe before turning on the television.

The explosion of the Cessna jet at Savannah/Hilton Head International Airport led the local news. A reporter with perfect blond hair stood outside the chain-link fence adjacent to the damaged jet, reporting that, fortunately, no one was on board when the Cessna exploded; however, one man was found dead at the scene. The body had yet to be identified. Police said they hadn't discounted the possibility of a terrorist bomb, but that was all they would say.

Tree lay down on the bed, mulling over what had happened, thinking about Rex, feeling guilty that he was somehow letting down his oldest friend in his time of need, intending to call Freddie, intending to order something to eat from room service.

He closed his eyes.

When he opened them again, there was a dog in the room. Where did the dog come from? Did he belong to one of the other guests and had somehow wandered in? Tree sat up as the dog hopped onto the bed. He was a sleek, long-legged, floppy-eared hound with large, moist eyes, white fur intersected with brown patches. He sank onto his haunches and turned his head, as though contemplating Tree.

"How are you doing, Tree?" the dog asked.

"Clinton?" Tree said. "You can talk?"

"Of course I can talk," Clinton said. "You don't look well, if you want me to be honest. Everything okay?"

"Not really," Tree said. "My best friend is in the hospital about to have heart surgery, I survived an explosion, and a couple of hours ago I found a dead body. Also, no matter how hard I try, I'm still missing you and feeling very sad about it."

Clinton said, "I miss you, too, Tree."

The dog sank down on the bed, stretched out, and nestled against him.

"Why didn't you tell me you can talk?"

"I'm sort of telling you now, aren't I?" Clinton said.

"How did you know I was here?"

"Nothing has changed," the hound said. "I'm always with you, never far away."

The dog's warmth next to him was like old times. He stroked at his soft fur. "I've been so miserable lately," Tree said.

"I know," the dog said, squirming closer to him. "I thought I'd come and cheer you up. I worry about you."

"You do?"

"Look at the trouble you're in again. Hiding out in a hotel room in Savannah. What's that about?"

"I know," Tree said. "I don't seem to be able to stay out of trouble."

"You're an old man, you shouldn't be doing these things."

"I'm dying," Tree said. "They think there's a problem with my heart. My kidneys, too. I'm supposed to pee into a plastic container. Only I haven't done it yet."

"No? Why not?"

"I've been trying to stay alive," Tree said.

The dog said, "Dying isn't so bad, although I do miss our walks on the beach."

"Me, too," Tree said. "I miss my friend, the pal who never lets me down."

The dog lifted his head. His eyes were moister than ever. "That hasn't changed. I'm still here for you, Tree."

There was a knocking on the door. Clinton's ears pricked up. "I'd better go," he said. "That's reality at the door."

"Don't go," Tree said.

"You've a long journey ahead of you," Clinton said. "Be careful, Tree—and don't worry so much about dying."

"I'll try not to," Tree said.

Clinton jumped off the bed. A voice outside said, "Tree. It's me. Open up."

Tree sat up. He was naked, crisscrossed by the shafts of early morning sunlight streaming through the window. Street sounds came from outside. There was no sign of a dog.

Tree opened the door. Freddie in jeans and a T-shirt, dropped the overnight bag she had been carrying and threw herself into his arms, kissing him hard on the mouth. Then she was inside, the door closed, tossing the overnight bag on the bed. "Were you talking to someone?" she said.

"I was sound asleep," Tree said.

"You must have been talking in your sleep."

"Dreaming," Tree said.

She gave him a pitying look and kissed him again. "I hope you're all right."

"I'm fine, now that you're here," he said.

"Tell me what's happening," Freddie said. "I heard on NPR on the way up here that a plane exploded at the Savannah airport. Please tell me you had nothing to do with that."

"I was there when it happened," Tree said.

She groaned.

As quickly as he could, Tree filled her in on the events of the past twenty-four hours. The flight to Savannah, the meeting in Ellis Square with his high school classmate, Dan Meade, suffering from CTE, the federal investigation of his involvement in online sports betting, his concern over the list he could no longer remember writing, the trip back to the airport, the explosion, and then the discovery of Pru Colt's body at the Meade house.

"And there was no sign of Dan Meade?"

Tree shook his head. "I searched through the house. He wasn't there."

"But his security guard and assistant are both dead, and someone blew up his jet."

"So, either Dan's dead somewhere and they haven't found his body, or he's hiding out."

"If he's in hiding why hasn't he tried to get in touch with you?" Freddie said.

"Maybe he can't."

"Let me take a look at that list," Freddie said.

Tree handed her the single sheet of paper. "He was very anxious that the people around him didn't see this," Tree explained. "As far as Kobus and Pru Colt were concerned, I was just an old high school pal their boss wanted to see."

"But you say you didn't even know each other that well in high school."

"I was surprised he even remembered me."

Freddie was studying the list. "One of the names is right here in Savannah."

"That's right. Harry Panama. What about him?"

"Let's go find this guy," Freddie said. "Maybe that's where Dan is."

"Right now?"

"Yes," Freddie said. "I brought you a change of clothes. Get dressed, and let's get at it."

"You're sure about this? You're just driven all night. Don't you want a nap?"

Freddie shook her head. "Come along, Tree," she said, rising from the bed. "The game's afoot!"

10

Harry Panama, according to Dan Meade's list, resided at number 210, one of the row houses along East Liberty Street. Tree parked the Mercedes adjacent to a line of impressive live oaks framing yet another of Savannah's many squares. Tree turned off the ignition. He sat there. Beside him, Freddie watched the townhouse. She said, "Okay, now what?"

"We wait," Tree said.

"Wait?"

"To see what Harry does."

Freddie looked at her husband in disbelief. "We're just going to sit here?"

"It's called a stakeout," Tree said.

"I don't care what it's called," Freddie said. "I don't want to sit here."

"That's what detectives do," Tree said. "They sit, and they wait."

"For what?"

"In this case for Harry Panama to make an appearance."

"And when he does?"

"We see what he does."

"I've got a better idea," Freddie said.

"What's that?"

"Let's knock on his door."

"And say what?"

"Let's tell him we saw his name on a list and are wondering why he's on it."

"That's too direct," Tree said.

"It's better than just sitting here," Freddie said. She opened the passenger-side door.

Tree said, "Where are you going?"

"To see if Harry's home."

Before he could stop her, Freddie was out the door. Tree swore and then followed her.

"Freddie," he called. "I don't think we should do this. Freddie…"

But she was already up the steps to the entrance. Tree sighed and went up behind her. Freddie was ringing the doorbell.

Tree's mind whirled, desperately thinking of what they could say to whoever answered the door. Unable to think of anything, short of what Freddie suggested—the truth. Presently, the door was opened by a gray-haired woman in a flowered dress.

Freddie said, "Good morning. We're here for Harry Panama."

The woman nodded and said, "I was beginning to think you wouldn't come."

Freddie barely hesitated before she said, "What would make you think that?"

"I just heard on the news that Mr. Meade is missing," the woman said. "It's a terrible thing that happened to those people, and now he's missing. It's just awful."

"Yes, it is," Freddie agreed.

"But you're here and that's a good thing; Harry said it should be like this. Business as usual, he says."

"Exactly," Freddie said brightly. "So here we are."

"Come in for a minute so I can get it for you," the woman said, stepping back and opening the door wider so that Freddie and Tree could enter.

They found themselves in a narrow hallway with an

oak staircase. "I'll be just a minute," the woman said. She turned and went down the hall and disappeared.

Freddie and Tree traded glances. To the right, just before the staircase, the hall opened into a living room. Heavy drapes were closed, shutting off outside light. Tree could barely make out the figure on the sofa.

As Tree stood there trying to adjust his eyes to the dimness, the figure stirred, a man raising his head, seeing two strangers in the hallway. "Mr. Panama?" Freddie said. "Is that you?"

"Yeah, that's me," Harry Panama said. He cleared his throat and sat upright, unshaven, balding, what little hair he had sticking out the side of his head. "What's going on?" he said to no one in particular.

Neither Freddie nor Tree said anything.

"I must have dozed off," Harry Panama said. He rose unsteadily to his feet. "I must have had a little too much wine at lunch. Makes me sleepy."

"It's only ten thirty in the morning," Freddie said.

Harry Panama smiled wryly. "I take an early lunch. Who are you, anyway?"

"Dan sent us over," Tree answered in the most authoritative voice he could muster.

"You heard from Dan? How's he doing? This business yesterday. Not good. The people he's got himself involved with, bastards all of 'em."

Freddie said, "Dan's concerned, Mr. Panama. He hasn't been himself lately, what with one thing and another. He wanted us to drop around, make sure you're all right."

In the dimness, Tree could see suspicion clouding Harry Panama's face. "Who did you say sent you over?"

Before Tree had to answer, the gray-haired woman reappeared. She carried a plain white envelope. Harry Panama said, "Irma, who are these people?"

The woman named Irma handed the envelope to Freddie. "When you get to Micanopy, tell Will that as far as we're concerned, we're finished, is that understood?"

"Yes," Freddie said, opening the envelope, seeing a white plastic credit-type card. "Do you mind if I tell Will why?"

"Why do you think? What happened yesterday. It's become too dangerous. These people. We don't know what's going on."

Harry Panama's voice rose, "Irma. You shouldn't be giving these two anything until we know who they are."

"Don't be ridiculous." Irma glared at Harry. "What would they be doing here, otherwise?"

"We should be going," Freddie said.

"Something's wrong," Harry called in a strangled voice. "Something's not right."

"Harry, stop this," Irma said in an agitated voice.

Harry wasn't listening. He fumbled with something beneath his loose-fitting shirt.

Tree had an instant to think to himself, No, he can't have a gun, before Harry had a gun.

Irma screamed, and then tried to seize the envelope from Freddie. "Give me that!"

Freddie yanked it away from her. Harry Panama waved the gun and yelled, rather incongruously, Tree thought, "Put your hands up."

"Tree," Freddie said, alarmed, "he's got a gun."

Welcome to my world, Tree thought, where everyone seemed to have a gun. Out loud he said, "I can see that."

Harry repeated, "Put your hands up!" just before he pulled the trigger. Nothing happened. Tree closed the gap between himself and Harry and smacked him on the side of the face. He grunted, dropped the gun and fell back on the sofa. Irma cried out and rushed to her fallen man.

Harry Panama made a loud groaning sound. Irma held his face in her hands, her eyes wild with fear. "Harry!" she shrieked. Then she turned and glared up at Tree, her face twisted in anger. "Who *are* you people?"

"We're trying to help Dan," Tree said. "Tell me what we're supposed to do with the envelope."

"Get out!" she yelled. "I'm calling the police."

"Irma, what do we do with the envelope? If you want to help Dan, tell me."

"You do what you always do with it. Will knows. Didn't Charade tell you anything?"

"Charade? Who is Charade?"

"Go to hell," Irma said. She rose imperiously. "I'm calling the police. Don't try to stop me."

She swayed out of the room. Tree looked at the gun in his hand. It was an automatic, but there was no clip in it.

Freddie called, "Tree, come on. Let's go."

Tree dropped the gun to the floor. From the sofa, holding the side of his face, Harry said something Tree couldn't understand.

"Tree," Freddie called again. "We have to go."

Tree returned to Freddie and together they went out the front door.

Outside, they hurried down the steps and over to where they had parked the Mercedes. Freddie was flushed, breathing hard. Tree got behind the wheel. Freddie slid in beside him. "He tried to shoot us," she was saying breathlessly. "He pulled the trigger. He would have shot us."

"Except the gun was empty," Tree said.

"My God, I can't believe what we just did," Freddie said. She looked at the card in the envelope as Tree started the motor. "What are we supposed to do with this?"

"Irma said that when we see Will we should tell him that she and Harry are through," Tree said.

"Whatever that means."

"Will Mickens in Micanopy," Tree said. "He's one of the names on the list."

Tree headed down the street, picking up speed. "Are we on the run?" Freddie asked. She sounded excited by the prospect.

"Not yet," Tree said out loud. To himself, he thought, It's only a matter of time.

11

They left the Mercedes with the parking attendant in front of the Cotton Sail and retreated to their room.

Freddie stretched out on the bed, and promptly fell into an exhausted sleep. Tree stepped onto the tiny balcony. Tourists crowded the narrow street below. Sunlight glinted off the spans of the Talmadge Memorial Bridge.

Back in his days at the *Chicago Sun-Times* Tree had spent time in Savannah for a travel story. The bridge was named after a Georgia governor named Eugene Talmadge, a rabid racist and dedicated segregationist, one of the most corrupt politicians in the state's history. When the original bridge was replaced in 1991, a name change was suggested, but the state legislature had decided to stick with Eugene, a memorial to a guy who enthusiastically supported the Ku Klux Klan and thought nothing of using state funds to attend the Kentucky Derby and to pay off friends and relatives.

A freighter with markings on its side indicating it had come from China made its way beneath the bridge, weighted down with containers piled high on its decks.

Watching the container ship pass, he didn't initially notice the activity on the street below. Then he saw the police cruiser pull up, followed by a second police car. There was nothing to say that the police were arriving in search of Freddie and him.

But still.

Tree went back into the room and grabbed their overnight bag, stuffed their clothing into it, and then gave the sleeping Freddie a shake. She squirmed a bit and said in a sleepy voice, "What is it?"

"Remember you were worried we were going to be fugitives?" Tree said.

"Yes," Freddie answered.

"You don't have to worry anymore—we are now fugitives."

"You don't know for certain that they are after us," Freddie said as they made their way down the stairs.

"Let's not take any chances," Tree said.

He had the overnight bag slung over his shoulder, thinking that if the police were after them it was probably because Irma or Harry Panama had called. But would they do that? And how would the police know where they were staying?

Still.

They reached the bottom of the stairs, and Tree said, "Take a deep breath and then let's walk out of here as calmly as we can."

He took her hand and opened the fire door and led the way into the lobby. A busload of Japanese tourists was checking in as Tree led Freddie across the lobby. Everyone chattered away, anxious to collect luggage and get checked in. The hotel staff looked harried. No one paid any attention to Freddie and Tree.

They went out the door and Tree saw more police cars and uniformed officers. Freddie gripped Tree's hand harder. The officers went right past them into the hotel.

They reached Ellis Square, crowded at this time of the afternoon with office workers, shoppers, and tourists.

Johnny Mercer hadn't moved since Tree last saw him. He still perched happily with his newspaper, propped against the fire hydrant.

"He can't possibly be very comfortable," Freddie said.

"This is where I met Dan seemingly a lifetime ago," Tree said.

"Well, he's not here now," Freddie said. "He's not here, and we're in trouble."

They sat on a nearby bench to catch their breath. "I hate to ask a mundane question like, What are we going to do now? But what are we going to do now?"

"I know you're about to suggest we go to the police and try to explain what's happened," Tree said.

"I'm not suggesting that at all," Freddie said. "Since you arrived in Savannah, a plane has blown up, a woman has been murdered, a well-known former football player under federal investigation has disappeared, and two people may have accused you—and me—of home invasion."

"That is a possibility," Tree said.

"Before we go to the police, who will promptly throw us in jail, we had better try to get to the bottom of what's going on." Freddie rummaged in the bag until she found the envelope with the card in it. "We have this card—and Will Mickens, who is on our list, is supposed to receive it, apparently."

"In a place called Micanopy."

"Then don't you think we should go to Micanopy?"

"Wherever that is," Tree said. "I asked Dan about Micanopy. He's never heard of it, and neither have I."

Freddie extracted her iPad from the overnight bag. It took her a moment to bring up Google Maps and type in the location. "It's just south of Gainesville," she announced.

"What would Dan want with someone living in northern Florida?"

"That's what he wanted you to find out," Freddie said.

"The question is, how do we get there? We can't go back to the hotel for the Mercedes, can we?"

"I don't think we should take the chance. But we could rent a car."

"Can fugitives from justice rent cars?" Freddie spoke while poking away again at her iPad.

"Sure they can," Tree said. "Fugitives have rights, just like everyone else."

"What do you know? There's an Enterprise Car Rental a seventeen-minute walk from here."

"See? Fugitives from justice can do just about anything."

"Can they get out of the trouble they find themselves in?"

"Easier to rent a car," Tree said.

12

The iPad's GPS said Micanopy was a three-hour drive in their rented white Ford Taurus. Less conspicuous, Freddie said. Everyone in Florida drove a white vehicle.

Traffic was light on southbound I-95. Freddie fiddled with the radio and found the local NPR station. Police were continuing their investigation of the Cessna explosion at Savannah/Hilton Head International Airport that killed one man. The FBI, as well as investigators from the National Security Agency, were also involved, officials not yet ruling out the possibility of a terrorist incident.

Police, according to NPR, were still looking for Daniel Meade, the jet's owner. The former Chicago Bears football great was under federal investigation for his alleged involvement in online gambling. As yet, they had not identified the body found in Meade's downtown Savannah home at the time he went missing.

"At least they didn't mention us," Freddie said.

"That doesn't mean anything," Tree said.

"So we could be suspects," Freddie said. "Fugitives. Tramps like us, baby we were born to run."

"You don't sound too upset," Tree said.

"I should be more upset, shouldn't I? I wonder what's wrong with me. Maybe it's age. I think to myself, what the heck? I might as well join my husband on the razor's edge."

"You think I live on the razor's edge?"

"Let's face it, Tree. For a guy who worries about dying, you do manage to find any number of ways to get yourself killed."

Micanopy advertised itself as "the town that time forgot," according to what Freddie was able to find on her iPad. Tree had to admit that it did seem to be located in a Brigadoon-like timelessness—at the end of a maze of back roads winding through a magical forested landscape draped in hanging moss and dappled with fading light.

"The town has been around since 1821," announced Freddie, "named after a Seminole chief. Only about six hundred people live here."

They passed a cemetery, neat rows of tombstones shaded by live oaks. There was a tiny white church, PARADISE, according to the sign. Tree said, "Aha, so this is where you find paradise."

"Your long search is over," Freddie said.

They came into Micanopy's main street, historic buildings on either side shimmering in evening gold. In the town that time forgot, you could almost hear the sound of horses' hooves. They parked their car and got out, stretching their legs.

They found a vintage clothing and jewelry store, a dog named Dakota, and a local woman named Lou. She showed them a photograph of the horse she had recently lost, and Tree, knowing what it was like to lose a beloved pet, shared a tear. Then Lou, the sort of no-nonsense woman who probably settled the area in the first place, got down to the business of extolling the town's virtues.

"You've arrived at what is believed to be the oldest inland town in the state. We attract tourists and fellas with beards who teach something or other at the University of Florida, about twenty minutes away.

"And outside town is the farm owned by Miss Marjorie Kinnan Rawlings, the place where she wrote *The Year-ling* and *Cross Creek*. Miss Rawlings loved this part of the country, and who could blame her? She had her problems, of course, men and booze. Being a person who has had far too many encounters with both those subjects, I identify with that woman, I truly do."

"What about Will Mickens?" Tree said.

Lou's face went blank. "What about him?"

"Is he in town?"

"You know Will Mickens?"

"A friend of mine asked me to look him up if we were coming through Micanopy."

"And who would that friend be?" Lou asked warily.

"Dan Meade. He and Will are old friends."

"You see that cemetery on your way into town?"

Freddie said, "Yes, we passed it."

"Well, that's where Will Mickens should be."

"I'm sorry to hear that," Tree said.

"Unfortunately, he's not there yet."

"I'm guessing this is a man you don't much like," Freddie said.

"I'm talking about a man no one in this town likes," Lou said. "A bastard if there ever was one."

"Sounds like someone we should stay away from," Freddie said.

"Not up to me to be telling anyone what they should or should not do," Lou said. "But if I were to be asked, that's what I would strongly advise."

"Staying away from him," Tree said.

"Far as you can," said Lou.

13

At the motel down the road where they checked in for the night, the Florida Gators room was available as was the Disney theme room. "You can have either one," said the ancient clerk behind the reception desk, though not so old that he didn't have faded tattoos up and down his left arm. "What's your preference, folks?"

Freddie wondered if there wasn't just a regular room. The ancient tattooed guy frowned. "Don't know what you mean by *regular*," he said in an irritated voice. "Folks come here ain't usually looking for *regular*. They look for something unique—and that's what we give 'em."

"We'll take the Disney room," Tree said, hoping to end the debate."

"Walt Disney *made* this state." The ancient tattooed guy said this in a way that suggested Tree and Freddie might think Walt didn't make the state.

"Hey, I'm a former Mickey Mouse Club member," Tree said.

The ancient tattooed guy just looked at him.

"Why? Because we like you," Tree said.

"Guess you think you're one of them funny fellas." The ancient tattooed guy didn't crack a smile.

A faded mural of Mickey Mouse taken from the "Sorcerer's Apprentice" segment of *Fantasia* filled most of a wall in their room. A black and white portrait of Walt in his heyday hosting *Walt Disney Presents* hung over the flat-screen television, the room's single concession to the twenty-first century.

Freddie came out of the bathroom naked, and Tree, marveling at the remarkable condition in which she kept herself, pulled her down on the bed and kissed her. She avidly returned his kiss, mumbling something about Bonnie and Clyde, and how being fugitives in a cheap motel room was kind of an aphrodisiac. "I don't know," Tree said, "I'm worried about my performance with Mickey looking down on me."

"I'm going to help you take your mind off Mickey," Freddie said.

"Then there's Walt over the TV," Tree pointed out. "I don't think he likes people having sex in front of him."

"Sorry, Walt," Freddie said to the photograph. "Just avert your eyes and hum, 'When You Wish Upon a Star,' and it'll all be over before you know it."

"Are you suggesting your husband is too fast?"

"I'm suggesting it's time my husband stops talking and gets to work," Freddie said, drawing him close.

And he did get to enjoyable work—until his cellphone went off. He groaned and might have ignored it had not Freddie insisted he swipe it open.

"Who's this?" the voice on the other end of the line said.

Tree recognized the uncertain rasp of Dan Meade. "It's me, Dan. Tree Callister."

"Who is this?"

"Dan, are you all right?"

"I've phoned this number," Dan said, sounding more confused, "but I don't know why."

"Dan, it's Tree Callister."

"Tree? Yes, Tree. High school." Dan sounded brighter. "It's good to hear your voice. How have you been?"

"Are you all right?"

"Of course. Why do you keep asking me that? Why wouldn't I be all right?"

"The police are looking for you, Dan. They think you've disappeared. Everyone is worried."

"I haven't disappeared, I'm fine," Dan said. "This is ridiculous."

"Your security guard has been killed. So has your assistant, Pru Colt."

"What? What are you talking about?" Dan's voice sounded panicky. "I have no idea what you're talking about."

"I'm trying to get to the bottom of why you created this list."

"List? What list?"

"The list you gave me when we met in Savannah. Can you remember anything about it? Anything that might help me?"

"I don't know, Tree." Dan's voice sounded weak again. "I'm very confused lately. Nothing makes sense."

"Do you recall anything about the list?"

"I don't know. I can't remember. Can't remember anything." His voice had become angry. "What the hell is wrong with me?"

"Is someone with you?"

Dan sounded desperate. "You have to tell me where you are."

"I'm trying to help you, Dan. Do you know someone or something named Charade? Does that mean anything?"

"Charade? I don't—"

The line went dead. Tree dropped the cellphone and slumped down on the bed. Freddie slid behind him, snaking her arms around his neck. "I got most of the conversation," she said. "What about Dan? Is he okay?"

"I'm not sure," Tree said. "He seemed very confused."

"I could tell that," Freddie said.

"What do you think?"

"I don't think we are going to solve this tonight," Freddie said. "So we should get back to the work we were doing before that phone call interrupted us."

"That's a very good suggestion," Tree said.

"I thought you might like it," Freddie said.

And for the next hour or so they forgot about everything but themselves.

14

Once they had showered and dressed and collected their things, they went out to the car. "So now what?" Freddie asked.

"We find Will Mickens," Tree said.

"According to our friend Lou, if we know what's good for us, we should stay away from Will Mickens."

"Except we don't know what's good for us," Tree said.

"In that case, let's drive around to the address on the list and have look."

Tree said, "I'm coming to the conclusion that the wrong person is the Sanibel Sunset Detective around here."

"It's only a suggestion," Freddie said. "Something we could do after I get coffee in me and we have some breakfast."

"A good investigator doesn't need breakfast," Tree said, starting the engine.

"Yes, but the investigator's wife does," Freddie said. "Otherwise, the investigator's wife gets grumpy."

"We can't have that," Tree agreed.

———

Cholokka Boulevard ran off First Street, not much of a boulevard, more a narrow lane running past the big house where Will Mickens lived. The Mickens house had been impressive at one point: two-story, wood framed, with a turret crowned by a pointed roof. But now it looked old and exhausted, threatening collapse under the weight of encroaching live oaks and magnolias.

Tree parked the Ford Taurus on First so that they had a view of the house. Not enough for the impatient Freddie.

"This isn't doing us any good," she said.

"It's a stakeout," Tree said.

"I don't like stakeouts," Freddie said.

"I get that impression," Tree said.

"There's far too much staking and not enough out."

"Patience is required," Tree said.

"I'll tell you what," Freddie said. "Why don't I wander over there and take a look around?"

"I don't want you doing that," Tree said.

"Why not? I'm a visitor to town out for a morning stroll. What's the harm in that? Right now, we don't know if there's even anyone home. We could be wasting our time watching an empty house."

Tree thought about this for a minute and said, "All right. Five minutes. Then come back so I know you're all right."

"I'll be fine." She patted his arm. "Don't worry about me."

"That's usually my line," Tree said.

"How times are changing," Freddie said.

She got out of the car. Tree watched her disappear around the corner.

He settled in his seat, moved around a bit to get more comfortable. He sat for a couple of minutes and then rolled down the window. The morning sounds of the cicadas chattering in the warming sun drifted into the car—the mating call of the male, he had read somewhere. Amazing what useless information he could dredge up sitting on one of these stakeouts. He didn't want to admit it to Freddie, but he hated waiting and watching almost as much as she did. He looked at his watch. She had been gone for at least five minutes.

Hadn't she?

He'd give her a little more time. He rearranged his position on the seat. That was better, more comfortable. He yawned. Damn. He really hadn't slept all that well last night. He yawned again. His eyes fluttered closed.

The sound of the male cicadas.

Calling.

"Tree. Tree, wake up."

Tree jerked awake and sat up. Freddie was by his window. She wasn't alone.

A man with white hair pushed back from a craggy, lined face bent down to get a better look at Tree. He wore suspenders, Tree noticed. The craggy-face man said, "Hello there, Tree. Hot out here. Makes a fella sleepy. Sleepy southern ways, I guess. Nice to make your acquaintance. Your wife, Freddie, is a charmer."

Freddie looked drawn and tense standing beside the craggy-face man. Tree glimpsed two other men coming up on the passenger side of the car. One of the men had a twelve-gauge shotgun. The other carried what looked like a Winchester repeating rifle.

The craggy-face man said in a friendly voice, "Name's Will Mickens. That's my house you've got your eye on."

"My wife and I love old houses," Tree said. "We're in town to take in some of the historic sites."

"Well, that house of mine, it's pretty damned historic, that's for sure," Will said.

"We're just visiting for the day," Tree said.

"Just visiting, eh?"

"That's right. Tourists passing through."

Will said, "We like to make tourists welcome here in Micanopy. You know the town was named after a great Seminole chief?"

"So we've heard," Tree said.

"Now that we've been introduced, and you know that we're friendly folks around here."

"Friendly folks with guns," Tree said.

"Hey, we're open carry around these parts," Will said. "Citizens got a right to protect themselves. You never know what kind of varmints might show up, try to destroy our way of life."

"That's right," Tree said. "You never know."

"Actually, I've been expecting you," Will said.

"You have?"

"Irma called, said you'd been around. Said she was a bit worried about you."

"No need to worry about us," Tree said.

"Irma and Harry were acting strangely," Freddie interjected. "They say they don't want to be in business any longer."

"Is that a fact?" Will glued on a smile and added, "No matter the circumstances, it's a pleasure to have the two of you visit us. Tell you what. How'd you like a little tour around the county?"

15

Will Mickens, from his position in the back seat of the Taurus, directed Tree along a series of flat, deserted county roads, straight lines through thickets of trees, gnarled branches twisting to form magnificent canopies. Behind them thundered a massive sand-colored military-type vehicle carrying Will's two henchmen and their guns.

"It's an armored, mine-resistant ambush-protected vehicle," Will explained. "What the army calls an MRAP. Reinforced steel doors. Pressurized cab. Improvised explosive device goes off on the road, you're gonna be well protected."

"Are there a lot of IEDs around Micanopy?" Freddie inquired.

"You never know," Will replied. "You never know about anything."

They came to a bridge over a narrow, placid waterway. A nearby sign declared that this was Cross Creek. Will ordered Tree to turn off the road, down a slight grade to the cabins situated among trees adjacent to the creek. Tree pulled to a stop. The MRAP stopped right behind him.

Tree kept his eyes on the side-view mirror, watching the two occupants of the military vehicle get out. He noticed they had their guns with them. Tree exited the car with Freddie, Will following. His craggy face broke out the grin he seemed to think made him appear friendlier. In fact, it scared Tree each time Will produced it.

"Beautiful, don't you think?" Will's raised hand took in the creek and the bridge and the surrounding forest.

"This here is the famous Cross Creek, the part of the country Marjorie Rawlings wrote about in her memoirs, taking the book's name from this here creek. *The Yearling* plumb reduced me to tears when I read it as a young boy."

He turned to Freddie. "What about you, Miz Callister? *The Yearling* make you cry?"

"I cried at the movie," Freddie said.

"There you go. Lots of emotion, even though I gotta admit my daddy had me out hunting deer by the time I turned ten. He didn't like no talk of *The Yearling*. Couldn't see what all the fuss was about. But it sure did affect me, no doubt about that. In a hard land, young Will Mickens realized he had himself a soft spot, he truly did."

"How about now, Will?" Tree inquired. "You still got that soft spot?"

"I'm an old softie, Tree." He nodded toward the two men with the guns. "But I'm afraid these boys ain't read *The Yearling*, and they are hard lads. If I got something unpleasant that has to be done, well, I call on them. Myself, I couldn't do some of the things need to be done."

"Hopefully, you're not planning anything unpleasant today," Tree said.

"That's a hope all right, Tree. I gotta agree with you, unpleasantness on a day like this, surrounded by nature's beauty, that's to be avoided, I would say. So why don't you just hand over that card and we can be done with business."

"Card? What are you talking about?" Tree asked.

"Tree, please don't disappoint an old rascal like myself by trying to pull something over on him, pretending you don't know things that you and I damn well know you know."

The atmosphere had tensed. Will held his shit-eating grin in place, but now it was rigid.

"I'm a private investigator," Tree said. "You're on a

list of names provided to me by Dan Meade. He's having some memory problems, and he hired me to investigate the people who are on that list and why."

Will snorted. "You don't look like no private investigator to me. You look more like an old fella should be signing up for that there Pilates or bingo, something like that."

"But here I am, Will, at Cross Creek, wondering why you're being so aggressive."

"That's because I'm kind of an aggressive fellow, Tree," Will answered.

"I thought you were a softie," said Tree.

"I want you to give me that card," Will said in a voice whose very softness suggested menace.

"The job Dan Meade hired me for was to make sure everything is all right," Tree said, a statement somewhat close to the truth. "You and your boys are not doing a very good job reassuring me that is the case."

"Well, sir, given your belligerence and refusal to cooperate, I may have to take that card away from you."

Without the help of his smile, Tree noticed, Will's face resembled a mask that would scare children of all ages on Halloween.

Only it wasn't Halloween.

"I wouldn't do that," Tree said.

"Why wouldn't you?" Will demanded.

"There's a problem," Freddie said, stepping forward.

"And what problem would that be?"

"Tree doesn't have the card."

Will glared hard at her. "The hell you say."

"I do say."

"You have it?" Will focused on Freddie.

"I know where it is," Freddie said.

"Where is it then?"

"Where I can find it when I need it," Freddie answered.

"Little lady, now's the time," Will said. "You need it."

"Freddie," Tree said. "Don't do this." He turned to Will. "She doesn't have it."

Will's eyes were hard on Freddie. "Do you?"

"Let's talk about this," Freddie said.

"Time for talk is over," Will said. He turned to the two men with the guns. "Ames, I want you to blow this sumbitch's head off."

Tree was having trouble swallowing. "That won't get you what you're looking for," he managed to say.

"That'll leave your grieving widow to provide it to us," Will said.

"Tree, I think we should give him the card," Freddie said.

"I don't think we should," Tree said.

"Ames, shoot him," Will ordered.

Ames, squat and unshaven, the jean shirt he wore barely containing the stomach overflowing his belt, squinted nervously at Will. "You sure you want me to shoot this fella, Will?"

"Wouldn't have asked you if I didn't want you to do it," Will replied. "Shoot him."

Ames didn't raise his gun. Instead, he looked at his partner, a tall, skinny, pimply-faced guy with the Winchester rifle. "What you thinking, Tab?"

Tab shrugged. "I dunno," he said. "I thought me and Ames signed on for scarin' people. I'm not so sure we signed up for shootin' 'em. That's a whole different thing."

"Okay, let's not get carried away," Freddie announced. "I'll give you the card."

All eyes were immediately on her.

"What's that supposed to mean?" demanded Will.

"It means I've got it," Freddie said. "As long as you don't shoot my husband."

"Don't seem to be a whole lot of enthusiasm in the shooting department," Will acknowledged.

"Freddie," Tree piped up. "Stop it. You don't have it."

"Don't listen to him." Freddie's gaze concentrated on Will. "I saw where my husband hid the card, thought he was making a mistake putting it there, and so I took it and put it in my purse for safekeeping. Here, let me show you."

Before Will or anyone else could object, Freddie pulled open her shoulder bag and began rummaging in it. "Here it is," she said.

But it wasn't the card she pulled out.

It was a gun.

16

Freddie pointed the gun at Will's head, a Glock, Tree guessed. "What's the cliché here?" she said in a surprisingly stern voice. "Oh, yes. Tell your men to put their guns on the ground. That's the one."

"Supposing my boys refuse," Will said.

"No, no," interjected Ames. "We're not refusing nothin'. We're puttin' our guns down."

Ames and the tall, skinny Tab laid their weapons down on the ground. Will groaned. "This'll teach me to use local workers."

"You damn well lied to us, Will," said Ames. "You said there would be no trouble. Instead, there's a crazy woman with a gun."

"You're right about that, I am a crazy woman, liable to shoot Will any time," Freddie said. "Tree, before I go completely off the deep end, please collect those guns."

Tree went over and picked up the shotgun and the Winchester, then moved back to Freddie and Will.

"Now what I want you to do, Will," Freddie went on. "I want the three of you to get in that truck and get out of here."

"You mean the MRAP," Will said.

"Call it anything you want," retorted Freddie. "Just get into it and drive away."

Will tried on a smile that didn't do a lot to relieve the irritation showing on his craggy face. "Damned crazy woman is right," he said. Nonetheless, he started moving toward the vehicle. His two men, looking immensely relieved, followed.

Will got into the vehicle while Tab climbed in the passenger side. Before he got in, Ames turned and addressed Freddie and Tree:

"That shotgun belonged to my daddy. He's down in Coleman serving a stretch for a crime he never committed. He gets out and finds I don't have his gun, he's gonna be mighty pissed. So if you could do me a big favor and just leave the gun against that tree over there, be much appreciated."

"I'll see what we can do," Freddie said.

Ames nodded and got into the truck beside Tab. Meanwhile, Will continued to cast scowls in the direction of Freddie and Tree. For a moment or two Tree feared Will might restart something. But then Will backed the MRAP onto the road and drove away toward Micanopy.

Tree turned to Freddie. She had dropped the gun to her side. She had gone white, shaking. Tree went over and lifted the gun out of her hand. "That was amazing," he said, wrapping his arms around her. She trembled against him. "What are you doing with a Glock?"

"Don't ask," Freddie said. "I got it after you called."

"You went out and bought a gun?"

"It's Florida," Freddie said. "It's like buying groceries."

"I can't believe you did that," Tree said.

"I can't believe *I* did that," she said.

"You don't even like guns," Tree said.

"I *hate* guns," she corrected. "I thought it would be safe in my purse, that it wouldn't get used if I had it."

"It got used," Tree said.

"What did you do with the card?"

He grinned and held her tighter. "I threw it away," he said.

She pulled back from him. "Are you serious?"

"You can see the trouble we're in because of it."

"Tree, a plane has blown up. A woman is dead, and a football player suffering from dementia has disappeared—and just now Will Mickens appeared to be willing to blow your head off in order to get hold of a plastic card you say you've thrown away."

"Maybe I shouldn't have used those exact words."

"You didn't throw it away?"

"In a manner of speaking I did—but the difference is, I know where I threw it."

"And where is that?"

Before Tree had to answer, his cellphone vibrated. It was Todd Jackson, Rex's elegantly mustached pal who had also become a good friend of Tree's. "Rex is out of surgery," Todd reported.

"That's a relief," Tree said. "How's he doing?"

"So far, so good," Todd said. "The doctors think he's come through it. But he's still asleep, so we'll see how it goes."

"I'm glad you're there, Todd. I'm only sorry I'm not."

"Speaking of that," Todd said. "The cops were around to see me. They wanted to speak to Rex, too, but, of course, he was unavailable."

Tree felt his stomach tightening again. "What did they want?" As if he didn't know.

"They wanted to know where you are."

"What did you tell them?"

"The truth—I don't know anything. And don't tell me. I want to be able to keep telling the truth."

"Did they say anything else?"

"Just a lot of questions about the last time I saw you."

"Thanks, Todd. I'm sorry to get you involved in this."

"Don't worry about me. Are the two of you all right?"

"We're okay," Tree said. "Listen, give Rex a hug for us, will you?"

"Will do. And Tree…"

"Yes?"

"I don't know what kind of trouble you've managed to get yourself into, but this time you've involved Freddie, so please, please be careful."

"The police are looking for us," Freddie surmised after Tree closed his phone.

"They came around wanting to talk to Rex," Tree said.

"How is he doing?"

"Todd says he's better, but not out of the woods yet. I'm just afraid he's not going to pull through."

"You should try to be a little more optimistic."

"Where dying is concerned, it's hard to be optimistic," Tree said.

Freddie did not disagree with him

17

By the time they made their way back to Micanopy, it was beginning to get dark. They parked a couple of streets away from Cholokka Boulevard.

Tree felt tired, as though he had run a marathon, cursing himself anew for expending what was left of his life over—what? The mystery of a list provided by an old high school friend who in fact was no old high school friend at all? Meanwhile, the police were after him while his oldest friend in the world lay possibly dying, and Tree wasn't there with him. What sort of asshole was he, anyway? As he had so often recently, Tree once again pondered the stupidity of the choices he had made.

Freddie looked at him and frowned. "Are you all right?"

"Sure," Tree said, pulling himself out of his reverie.

"It's as though you're not here," Freddie said.

"Just thinking about the waste of all this, I guess."

"Waste?" Freddie looked surprised—and vibrantly alive. Waving off thugs with a gun appeared to have energized her. She was ready for more. There was no waste, only the promise of more excitement.

"Come on," she said, opening the passenger-side door. "Don't be so down on yourself. No time for second thoughts."

Yes, no second thoughts. Not for now. Freddie was right. He had to get that card.

They left the car and walked along to where they previously had parked on First Street. Wooden posts pounded into the ground preventing cars from parking on the lawn were all but lost among ferns exploding with pointed leaves. Tree stopped.

Freddie said, "Is this where you left it?"

Tree didn't answer. He bent down running his hand under one of the ferns and recovered the plastic card. "Just where I left it," he announced proudly.

"What a detective," Freddie said.

Tree rose to his feet, grunting with the exertion. "Let's get out of here," he said.

"There is one more name on the list," Freddie said.

"Yes, there is," Tree agreed.

"A.T. Kamala. On Connecticut Avenue in Washington."

"What are you suggesting?"

"For now, we find a place to stay, get some rest, and then decide on next steps in the morning."

Tree was about to agree when his cellphone began to vibrate. He didn't recognize the number on the readout but swiped it open anyway.

"Tree? Is that you?" said a familiar voice.

"Dan?"

Beside him, Freddie whispered, "See if you can find out where he is."

Dan said, "Tree, I've been worried about you."

"I'm okay, Dan. How are you?"

"I've been through a bad spell, no doubt about it. It's been a little nuts; I haven't been myself lately. But I'm feeling better now and thought I'd better check in with you."

"I'm relieved to hear your voice, Dan. Where are you?"

"I'm somewhere safe, Tree. That's all I'd better say right now. A lot of people are looking for me, and it's just not a good time. Better to lie low for a while. But I wanted to get in touch with you now that I'm feeling better. Tree? Did I tell you I'm feeling better?"

"Yes, you did, Dan."

"I'm concerned about that list. I need to know what progress you've made."

"I've checked the names in Savannah and now in Micanopy, Florida. I've been in touch with Will Mickens."

Silence on the line.

"Dan? Is that name familiar to you? Do you know who I'm talking about?"

"No."

"Will Mickens is on your list."

"Will? Will Mickens?" Dan sounded alarmed.

"I'm trying to decide what to do about the last name. A.T. Kamala. In Washington. Do you know who I'm talking about?"

"Of course I know who you're talking about. You think I'm crazy?"

"So tell me about him."

"I don't know what you're doing with that bastard. A.T. is the world's worst son of a bitch, that's who A.T. is." Dan's voice was agitated, pitched high. "Whatever you do, Tree, don't have anything to do with him. You understand?"

"But he's on your list."

"Are you out of your mind? I don't know what the hell you're talking about."

"Dan, what are you saying?"

"For God's sake, man, wake *up!*" Dan was yelling into the phone now. "That bastard wants to *kill* me. That's what he's trying to do. He's trying to kill me. He blew up my jet, *damn it*, killed my assistants."

"Why, Dan? Why is A.T. Kamala doing these things?"

"For God's sake, there's no point talking to you. You're speaking in tongues, Tree, spouting gibberish. All these years and you don't understand anything. It's a good thing I'm feeling better—and I *am* feeling better, I really am. Everyone says so. If I wasn't feeling better, and I am, I've never felt better."

"Dan..."

"Shut up! Just shut the hell up. I don't have time for this. I paid good money to find out about that list, and so far you haven't given me anything. You're a loser, Tree. You always were a loser. In high school you were a loser. Everyone said so. Find out about the list, loser. Goddamn loser!"

The line went dead, leaving Tree staring at his cellphone. Freddie said, "Tree."

Tree said, "He hung up on me."

"Tree," Freddie repeated.

He looked up. Three men had materialized out of the darkness. They wore aviator glasses and sheriff's deputy uniforms. All three held Glock automatics pointed at Freddie and Tree. One of the deputies said, "You two are under arrest."

18

The deputies wore stiff-brimmed regulation campaign hats that made them look like Smokey the Bear. Comical, Tree thought, except no one was laughing. As one of the officers handcuffed him, Tree had the presence of mind to ask: "Why are we under arrest, officer?"

"Shut up," came the reply.

By now a couple of cruisers had pulled to a stop. No flashing lights, Tree noticed. Nothing to alarm the neighbors.

"I have a right to know what we're being arrested for," Tree said.

"You have the right to get into that cruiser back there and keep your mouth shut," said the officer, taking him by the arm and pushing him forward.

Another officer held the back door open for him. He said, "Watch your head," and then helped him bend forward so that he could cram into the backseat. The officer then crowded in beside him.

Tree said, "What's this all about?"

"Didn't the officer tell you to keep quiet?" said the deputy beside him. He was sweating under the armpits. His body odor filled the car. Tree looked at him. "You look familiar," he said.

"Do I?" replied the officer. He removed his aviator glasses.

"Ames," Tree said.

Ames grinned and said, "Thanks for leaving my shotgun out at Cross Creek, Mr. Callister. Otherwise, my daddy would've killed me soon as he got out of Coleman."

"Always happy to help out members of the law enforcement community," Tree said.

"Yeah, we're kinda shaky members of that community, I would say, but nonetheless your support is appreciated, Mr. Callister."

The holding cells at the Alachua County Sheriff's department stank of disinfectant, an all-too-familiar smell to Tree. Freddie was placed in an adjacent cell. He could see her through the bars. She looked more curious than upset, this being her first stay in a cell. Needless to say, this was not Tree's first rodeo. For a sleuth who was supposed to solve crimes, rather than being accused of committing them, he had spent far too much time in jails.

Beside Freddie, a young woman slumped against the wall. She was blond, wearing a short skirt and black stockings. Her mascara ran down her cheeks as she wept and called to the young man lying on the floor not far from Tree. The young man wore a T-shirt and jeans. A muscular arm was thrown across his eyes, as he tried to sleep.

"Aaron," the blond woman in Freddie's cell bleated. "Aaron, talk to me for God's sake."

"Will you shut up, Alice?" Aaron mumbled. "I'm trying to sleep. I don't feel well."

"Aaron," Alice, the blond girl, cried. "I don't want to be here. I want to go home."

"Then you shouldn't have driven the car the wrong way down a one-way street," Aaron said.

Freddie passed Alice a tissue. Alice noisily blew her nose and then resumed weeping. "I can't believe this, I can't believe I'm in jail," she moaned. "My parents are going to kill me, they really are."

"If it's any consolation, I can't believe it, either," Freddie said.

Alice dabbed the tissue at her eyes and stared at Freddie as though noticing her for the first time. "But you're old," she exclaimed. "What's an old person doing here? They don't put old people in jail, do they?"

"Apparently, they do around here," said Freddie.

On the floor, Aaron rolled onto his side and groaned. "Alice, will you keep quiet?" he called. "There's a lawyer on his way. He's gonna get us out."

"When?" Alice cried. "When's he coming, Aaron? I can't stand this. I can't!"

This was followed by more tears.

Deputy Ames appeared, jangling a cluster of keys. He was no longer wearing his Smokey the Bear hat. He unlocked the door to Tree's cell and motioned to him. "Sheriff wants to see you," Ames said.

"Me?" Tree said, standing.

"Now I'm not gonna handcuff you, Tree," Ames said. "You're not going to try to escape or anything like that, are you?"

"What happens if I do?" Tree said, exiting the cell.

"Hell, then I'd have to shoot you," Ames said. He was smiling when he said it.

Behind him, Aaron groaned again and rolled onto his back. "I feel awful," he announced to an uncaring world.

Alice wailed even louder.

19

Tree expected to be taken to an interrogation room. That was the drill to which he had become all-too ac- customed. The stumblebum gumshoe experienced in the ways of criminal incarceration. What would his mother think?

But instead of an interrogation room, Deputy Ames led him along a cinderblock hallway to a fire door. He stopped Tree and produced a pair of handcuffs. "Let me see those hands in front of you," he said.

"What's this about? I thought you weren't going to hand- cuff me."

"Sheriff's orders. Gimme your hands and quit asking questions." Deputy Ames looked a trifle nervous as Tree reluctantly held out his hands. Quickly, Ames snapped the handcuffs around his wrists. How many times had this hap- pened to him? Tree mused. Too many times—far too many.

Ames pressed his hip against the fire door and it snapped open. "Just remember, I didn't have nothin' to do with this," he said.

"To do with what?" Tree demanded, not liking the sound of this.

Deputy Ames didn't answer. Instead, he opened the fire door wider and pushed Tree out.

Tree stumbled forward into a parking lot. The intimidat- ing bulk of the MRAP stood out in the darkness. Standing beside the vehicle, bareheaded, but now dressed in a sheriff's uniform was Will Mickens. He held a black, gun-like object.

"Don't tell me you're the sheriff," Tree said.

"Didn't I mention that?"

"You must have forgot," Tree said.

"Been the sheriff here in Alachua County for twenty years now," Will said. "People around these parts love me."

"I'm sure they do," Tree said.

"They love me 'cause I bring law and order to this county. When I am not strong, this county is not safe. Lack of strength means weakness and that means the county is not safe, and I have promised the citizens of this county that their lives will not be in jeopardy." He pounded his fist against the side of the MRAP. "That's why we got this baby right here from the U.S. Military. Citizens need to feel safe. This makes them feel safe. I make them feel *real* safe."

"I'm sure your service to the county is greatly appreciated," Tree said.

Will closed in on Tree. There was no sign of the friendly, shit-eating smile tonight. "You know how our encounter this afternoon made me look, Tree? It made me look weak."

"I didn't know you were the sheriff here," Tree said. "If Freddie had known, she never would have pointed a gun at you, even though you were threatening to blow my head off."

"In front of my deputies, too," Will continued. "I can't have that. I must be strong. I cannot be weak."

He waved the weapon he was holding. "You know what this is?"

"Some sort of gun, I would say." Tree was shivering, even though it was a warm night.

"I call it Dr. Will's Law and Order Medicine. Patients who receive a dose of this medicine, why, more often than not, it straightens 'em right up.

"Other law enforcement types, fellas more sophisticated than this poor, old sheriff, they call it a Taser Electronic Control Device. Have you heard about it?"

"Yes," Tree croaked.

"The way it works, you fire at the suspect—that's you in this case—and there are barbed electrodes on the ends of two wires. The wires transmit electrical impulses, twelve hundred volts of muscle-locking electricity. Essentially, what you're doing, you're overriding the electrical impulses that control the muscles. Immobilizes the suspect—that being you, Tree. Nice thing about it from my perspective, it leaves no marks. You can administer a dose of my medicine without leaving telltale cuts and bruises."

"You're not going to do this, Sheriff," Tree said in a voice trembling a lot more than he intended it to.

That produced one of Will's shit-eating grins. "No, of course not, Tree."

Tree was vaguely aware of a popping sound followed by the *tick-tick-tick* of the electrical pulse. He had an instant to see gossamer-thin wires arching toward him. His entire body was racked with an intense pain, unlike anything he had ever experienced. He heard someone screaming. By the time he realized that the screams were his, he was down on the pavement, his body jerking spasmodically.

Tree could hear Will's calm, reasonable voice coming from a distance. "Now, ordinarily I tase an uncooperative suspect for thirty seconds, but I only gave you a ten-second jolt, Tree, because I know you're going to cooperate with law enforcement, namely myself."

Tree tried to say something; couldn't get the words out, the Taser having turned his brain to mush. He was aware of Will bending over him, yanking his body around so that he could get at the wallet in his back pocket. He was breathing hard as he straightened up.

Tree watched as Will thumbed through the wallet until he found what he was looking for: the white plastic card from Harry Panama in Savannah. He nodded with satisfaction as he popped the card into his shirt pocket and then threw the wallet to the pavement.

"Now we got that particular problem solved." Will held the Taser gun like a trophy. "But you know, I believe I should give you one more dose of Dr. Will's Law and Order Medicine, a further reminder that you don't come to Micanopy and mess with Sheriff Will Mickens. You just don't do that."

This time Tree didn't see anything. But abruptly gut-wrenching pain again shot through him. His body involuntarily leapt off the pavement, followed by more disembodied screams.

But then, over the sound of his howling, he heard something else. A voice, demanding, "What's going on here?"

Through his haze of pain, Tree thought he saw lawyer T. Emmett Hawkins coming toward him.

No, Tree thought. It couldn't be. Not here. Next thing, he would be listening to a talking dog.

20

Hold it right there," Will Mickens snarled as T. Emmett Hawkins ambled forward. It was a dainty, elegant amble, appropriate for a man who wore a bow tie and a linen suit even at this late hour in a sheriff's department parking lot. "You, my friend, are interfering with police business."

"On the contrary," Hawkins announced in the smooth southern cadence that brought a hush to many a courtroom—and that saved Tree's bacon on more than one occasion. "I believe I am preventing my client from being the subject of unwarranted police abuse."

"Your client?" That stopped Will.

"I am T. Emmett Hawkins, sir. Attorney at law. You have three more of my clients currently occupying jail cells inside. I presume you are Will Mickens, the sheriff of this county."

"I am that man, certain enough," Will said, puffing out his chest, trying to regain the sense of authority lesser men had difficulty hanging onto when confronted by T. Emmett Hawkins. "You represent them stupid drunken kids?"

"That so-called stupid kid is the son of Madison Starke Perry, state senator and a good friend. I've come to bail out him and his girlfriend and take them home."

"You can take them kids, but this sumbitch"—he waved the Taser gun in Tree's direction—"him and his wife stay right here in my jail."

Hawkins said, "Sheriff, I know you."

"Do you now?" Will sounded even more belligerent.

"A man who is, I believe, under investigation for various misdeeds. It looks like I will be able to add this episode to the growing list of grievances."

"This here suspect was attempting to escape custody," Will said.

"This man is handcuffed," responded Hawkins.

"We can fix that in a jiffy," Will said. "Turn around Mr. Callister."

Tree turned and a moment later, he felt the relief of metal being lifted from around his wrists. "There you go," Will said, tucking the handcuffs into his belt.

"What is my client charged with?" Hawkins demanded.

"We brought him in for questioning," countered Will.

"Then if you're not going to charge Mr. Callister or his wife, I am taking them out of here. If you don't release them, then I will contact Judge William Bartram Cowkeeper, and you will have to deal with him."

By now, Tree had regained some feeling in his muscles. The pain was subsiding. He had managed to get to his knees, and was trying to clear his head. Hawkins stepped over and put his hand out. "Let me help you up, Tree."

Hawkins, surprisingly strong for a man seemingly frail, lifted Tree to his feet. "You all right?" he asked.

"I think so," Tree said.

Hawkins swung angrily around to confront Will. "This is an abomination what you have done to this man," he said, his face reddening. "It's nothing less than torture."

"He's an escaping fugitive," Will insisted. "Fella's lucky I didn't shoot him. Few years ago, before the Taser come along, I would've."

"What have you done with Mr. Callister's car?" Hawkins demanded.

Will appeared taken aback by the question. "You ain't accusing me of car theft are you?"

"I'm asking you a question."

"It's parked around the corner," Will responded. "Not trying to hide it or anything."

"Then will you please get the keys, and while you're at it, release Ms. Stayner from the cell."

"You're lucky I am a forgiving type of man," Will said with fading authority; he had met his match and been bested. He threw Tree a nasty scowl, and then turned on his heel. Tree called to him, "Hold on a minute, sheriff."

Will stopped and turned. Tree went over and plucked the card from his pocket. "I'll take that back."

Will's scowl grew deeper. "You got no right to that."

"Is that Mr. Callister's property?" Hawkins demanded.

"It's mine," Tree said.

"Then under the law, sheriff, you must return a citizen's property, unless you charge him with a crime."

Will looked as though he would have liked nothing better than to tear Tree's head off. Instead, he heaved a deep breath and disappeared inside.

Tree shoved the card into his pocket and then slumped against Hawkins. "How did you ever get here?" he said in an exhausted voice.

"I have a place just outside Gainesville. Those kids in there, the boy's father is an old school friend of mine. He phoned me an hour ago and said his son was in trouble. You can imagine my surprise when I walked in and found Freddie sitting in a cell. The deputy was kind enough to inform me that you were out here being tortured."

"It's a good thing you arrived when you did," Tree said.

The door opened and Freddie came out, looking relieved when she saw Tree. "Are you all right?"

"I'm fine," he said, "although I can now tell anyone who asks what it's like to be tased."

"You fool," Freddie said, coming into his arms. "You absolute fool."

"I'm not going to ask what's going on," Hawkins said. "Let's get the two of you out of here before the sheriff in there changes his mind."

"I've got the car keys," Freddie said.

"If you have any plans to stay around the Gainesville area, I would abandon them if I were you," Hawkins said.

"No plans," Tree said.

"Good. I'd better get inside and see to those kids."

Tree shook Hawkins's hand. "Thanks, Emmett."

"Glad I happened along when I did." Hawkins eyed Tree sorrowfully. "I do have a question for you."

"Sure, Emmett. What is it?"

"Is there anywhere in the world you go that you *don't* get into trouble?"

"The answer to that question is no," Freddie said.

21

The clerk at the Comfort Inn announced she had one room left with a queen-size bed. That would be eighty-nine dollars plus tax.

The room in shades of brown was similar to thousands of other hotel rooms just off the highways crisscrossing America, including the noisy air conditioner and the television Tree could not figure out how to work. He threw the remote on the bed and then lay stretched out on his back, trying to relieve the soreness in his muscles. Failing. He had read somewhere that the effects of the Taser wore off quickly.

Ha.

Freddie emerged from the bathroom and flopped beside him. "How are you doing?"

"Sore."

"I was just thinking about how Sheriff Will and his deputies would have known we were back in Micanopy."

"Maybe one of them saw us," Tree suggested.

"Or maybe someone told him."

"Dan Meade?"

"Who else?"

"I have to think it was coincidence," Tree said.

"I thought private detectives didn't believe in coincidence."

"Who told you that? Private detectives are big believers in coincidence."

"However it happened, we're in more trouble than ever," Freddie said. "Thank goodness for small miracles—

in the form of T. Emmett Hawkins, a most unlikely guardian angel."

"I'm not sure what to make of Dan."

"As in, he may not be suffering from dementia after all?"

"He says he's better, but when you talk to him, he doesn't seem well at all."

"Unless he's putting it on," Freddie said. "If people think he's not capable of taking care of himself—well, that helps Dan, doesn't it?"

"I suppose, but then why hire me?"

"Irrational guy hires old high school pal to chase a meaningless list. If you're trying to demonstrate to the world that you're mentally unfit, that could be helpful."

"What are you saying?" Tree said. "That no one in their right mind would hire me?"

"Did I say that?" Freddie, all innocence.

Tree took the list out of his pocket and spread it on the bed. Freddie propped herself up on an elbow. "What are you doing?"

"Thinking," Tree answered.

"Uh-oh," Freddie said. "That's not a good sign."

"We have to go to Washington."

"Because?"

"Because A.T. Kamala is on the list, and apparently he's in Washington."

"That's it?"

"Maybe I want to reassure myself that this isn't something Dan cooked up to make everyone believe he's crazy."

"Okay. Let's go."

"You want to go to Washington? Just like that?"

"Just like that," Freddie answered.

"And to think, less than an hour ago as I lay there being tased in a parking lot, I promised myself that if I survived,

I would go home and never ever tell anyone that once I was a private detective."

"Shows how tough you are," Freddie said.

"Getting tased reminded me that I'm actually a weak, sniveling coward."

"You were thinking rationally," Freddie said. "I'm the one who's turned into this the wild and crazy danger junkie."

Tree said, "Speaking as one junkie to another…"

"Yes?"

"You look kind of sexy lying there like that."

"Aren't you sore?"

"Not that sore. Besides, haven't you heard? After being tased, victims have this unquenchable desire for sex."

"I hadn't heard that."

"It's been established scientifically."

"Tree, we're both dead tired. This is no time for hanky-panky."

"Hanky-panky? I haven't heard it described like that for a long time."

"Tree, stop it. Tree…" Freddie groaned. "We're too old and too tired."

She groaned again. Not so old, not so tired after all.

22

The sound of scratching woke Tree from a deep sleep. He sat up, disoriented. It was pitch black. Where was he? Of course, a hotel room off a highway somewhere in Florida. The scratching continued. It seemed to come from the door.

Tree got up and went over to open the door. A hound dog with soft ears and spindly legs cocked his head at Tree.

"Clinton," Tree said, happily. "There you are. Where have you been?"

The dog wagged his long tail and then trotted off down the shadowy hall. Tree stepped out, calling, "Clinton. Come here, boy. Clinton…"

But the dog kept going away. Tree started after him, calling again. It grew darker. Tree could just make out Clinton in the distance. "Clinton," he called. "Come back here."

A shaft of light came into view. Clinton darted toward it. Tree hurried after him. In the light, he could see a figure slumped forward at a table, a wispy line of smoke rising from the cigarette between his fingers. A shot glass was on the table, a whiskey bottle beside it.

The man wore a white dinner jacket. Sad, coal-black eyes set in a lined face that had been around many blocks squinted through curling cigarette smoke. "Hey, kid," the man said with an ironic smile. "Don't mind me, I'm waiting for a lady."

"I'm looking for a dog," Tree said.

"She's coming back," the man said, staring into his glass. "I know she's coming back." He lifted his sad eyes to Tree. "What's that you say? A dog?"

"Have you seen him? He answers to the name of Clinton."

"It's December 1941 in Casablanca, what time is it in New York?"

"I don't know," Tree said. "I'm not wearing a watch. But it's late, and I can't find my dog."

"I'll bet they're asleep in New York. I'll bet they're asleep all over America."

"They're asleep in Florida, that's for sure," Tree said. "I'm dead tired. As soon as I find Clinton, I'm going back to bed."

"Clinton?" The man shook his head. "I've seen a lot of gin joints in a lot of towns in the world, but I don't think they got any dogs."

"It's you, isn't it?"

"That depends on who 'you' is."

"You're Bogart—Bogie. I grew up watching you, wanting to be you."

"You got the wrong guy, pal. My name is Rick, and I've just had my heart broken so you don't want to be me."

"Yes, yes," Tree said, trying to keep the excitement out of his voice. "You're Rick in *Casablanca*. But you're not *really* Rick. You're Bogie. You're tough without a gun."

"Yeah, fine, have it any way you want, kid." The man who insisted he was Rick sat back with a resigned sigh and lit another cigarette. "My daddy taught me to never disagree with a guy looking for a dog."

"You shouldn't be smoking," Tree said. "Smoking cigarettes will kill you."

"A bullet will kill you, kid. A broken heart sure as hell will kill you. I'm not so sure about the cigarettes." He blew gray-blue smoke into the air and reached for the shot glass. He downed its contents in a single gulp.

"Also, whiskey isn't good for you either," Tree said.

"Take some advice from me. You're better off without it."

"My daddy always told me never take advice from a guy looking for his dog," Rick said. He lifted the whiskey bottle and poured himself another drink.

"You don't know this," Tree said, "but the booze and the cigarettes are going to kill you at the age of fifty-seven."

"That's where you've got it all wrong," Rick said. "Nothing can kill me. I'm going to live forever. I'm immortal. You, on the other hand, no one remembers you now. What do you think's going to happen once you're dead?"

"Not much, I suppose," Tree said.

"You got that right," Rick said. "How much time do you think you have left?"

"That's what I'm afraid of," Tree admitted. "It's what I think about all the time. The fact that I'm closer to the end than the beginning."

"So you might as well have a drink, kid. The world is about three drinks behind. You look as though you're at least five. No matter what you do, no matter how careful you are, you're gonna die, anyway. The way I hear it, they come after the guys with dogs first."

"I love Clinton," Tree said sadly. "I miss him every day."

"A dog lover." Rick's mouth twisted distastefully. "You call yourself a tough guy? Moping around over a mutt? Dames who put a .45 slug through your heart and laugh as you bleed out on the side of the road, now you're talking despair. But a mutt? Give me a break will you? What kind of a detective can't get over a mutt?"

"I'm a detective who shouldn't be a detective," Tree said.

"Get out of it, kid. Become a dog walker or something. You seem better suited for that."

"I tried to retire after I'd been shot twice, but that didn't work out so well," Tree said.

"Wait a minute." Rick paused, the whiskey bottle hovering over the shot glass. "You were shot?"

"Twice. What? You think that's impressive?" Tree said.

"Are you kidding? A good detective doesn't get himself shot once, let alone twice. You're supposed to shoot people. You're not supposed to get shot. "

"Anyhow," Tree continued. "I'm back in business and on a case."

"Does it involve dogs?" Rick asked.

"People are dead. My wife is in danger. The police are probably after me. Every time I try to get out of trouble I end up in more of it."

"I don't take advice, kid, but I do give it." Rick paused to light another cigarette. The smoke had become so thick Tree could hardly see him.

Rick said, "Quit chasing dogs you're never going to find. Stop feeling sorry for yourself. Get out there and solve the case."

"Okay," Tree said. "That's good advice, I guess. Thanks."

"Any time, kid." Rick was all but lost in the dense cigarette smoke. "What I can't figure, if you'd wanted to be more like me, why aren't you more like me?"

"I came to understand that what works on the Warner Bros. backlot in shades of black and white, doesn't work so well in real life. At least it didn't for me."

"Kid, I don't understand what you're talking about, but whatever happens, good luck."

Rick's voice began to fade. The smoke grew thicker.

"I can hardly hear you," Tree said.

"What's that you're playing?" he called faintly.

"I'm not playing anything."

"You played it for her, now play it for me."

"What?" Tree said.

23

You were talking in your sleep again," Freddie said the next morning as they dressed after their showers.

"What was I saying?"

"You were calling for Clinton."

"He led me to Humphrey Bogart," Tree said.

"I know," Freddie said.

"You know?"

"You were mumbling something about Rick in *Casablanca*."

"Yes, Bogie was in a white dinner jacket, just like in *Casablanca*."

"I couldn't make it all out, but you kept telling Bogart you are afraid of dying."

"I *am* afraid of dying," Tree said.

Freddie embraced him. "Humphrey Bogart and Clinton," she said softly. "You poor man."

"I'm all right," Tree said.

"I wonder."

"It's just that everything is dying around me. Dogs. Friends. It takes a toll, at least it does on me."

"We can go home," Freddie said, breaking away to get a better view of this contradictory man who was her husband, this surprisingly complex guy who feared death yet regularly managed to nearly get himself killed.

"We don't have to do this," Freddie went on. "We can go back and live a more normal life."

"Right after we are released from police custody," Tree said.

"There is that," Freddie said.

"I don't think a normal life is in the cards right now. Whatever a 'normal' life is."

"I think it's something that existed before you became a detective."

"Let's get out of here and find some breakfast," Tree said. "That's normal enough, isn't it?"

She agreed it was.

———

They drove along searching for a Panera restaurant, preferred by Freddie. But this part of Florida was not big on Panera. They settled instead for Tree's favorite, Cracker Barrel, a Norman Rockwell fantasy of homespun rural America complete with rocking chairs out front, country music on the sound system, and a smiling grandmother moonlighting as a waitress pouring coffee and taking breakfast orders.

"You only like it because they sell DVDs of old *Gunsmoke* episodes." Freddie said.

"James Arness as Matt Dillon knew how to handle things," Tree said.

"Did he? I'm not so sure about that. I mean the big galoot settled everything with a gun and never slept with Miss Kitty, even though she was a saloon girl who probably slept with a lot of other men."

"Hey, I can't stay in the same Cracker Barrel if you're going to criticize Marshal Dillon or impugn the integrity of Miss Kitty."

"Matt Dillon had problems with sex is all I'm saying," Freddie said. "And Kitty was a whore."

Tree reacted in mock horror. "Careful, woman. Language like that will get us kicked out of Cracker Barrel."

After being seated in the airy dining room near the fireplace, they ordered the breakfast oatmeal, and the grandmother-turned-waitress poured coffee. Tree's cellphone sounded. It was Todd Jackson. "Thought I'd better give you a call and update you," he said.

"How's Rex doing?"

"Not so good," Todd said. "They thought he would have regained consciousness by now, but he hasn't."

Tree was silent, attempting to gather his thoughts. Except there were no thoughts to gather, only panicky concern about his old friend. "What are the doctors saying?"

"Not much. I get the impression they are crossing their fingers and praying that he comes around."

"All right, Todd. We're driving back this morning."

Now it was Todd's turn for the long pause. Finally, he said, "Uh, Tree, that might not be such a good idea."

"Why is that?"

"The police have been around a couple of times looking for you," Todd said. "They would like to have a 'talk.' That's the way they put it."

"I see."

"Knowing you, the last thing you probably want right now is the police."

"There is that," Tree said.

"To be honest, there's not much you can do except maybe end up in police custody, and that isn't going to help Rex."

"Thanks for this, Todd," Tree said. "I'll have a talk with Freddie, and we'll decide on next steps."

"Stay in touch," Todd said. "I'll call you as soon as I hear anything from the doctors or if he regains consciousness."

Their oatmeal arrived. The grandmother-waitress refilled their coffee cups. Tree stared at his cereal. "No change?" Freddie asked.

Tree shook his head. "Rex still hasn't regained consciousness."

"Do you want to go home?"

"I don't know what to do," Tree said.

"Eat your cereal," Freddie said. "I'm going to the ladies room."

The grandmother posing as a waitress came by and frowned down at Tree. "You've hardly touched your oatmeal," she said.

"I guess I don't have much of an appetite this morning," Tree said.

"You should eat. Breakfast is the most important meal of the day."

"Actually, it isn't," Tree said. "There was a report in the *New York Times* recently. There's no evidence that breakfast is any more important than any other meal."

The waitress-grandmother's frown only deepened. "That's that Yankee newspaper, right?"

"Well, yes, it's a New York newspaper."

"There you go. What do they know about anything? Eat your breakfast, son."

How could you argue with a grandmother who called you son? Freddie returned as he finished the oatmeal. She carried a DVD. "No episodes of *Gunsmoke*, unfortunately. But here's something even better."

She placed the DVD in front of him. Cary Grant and Audrey Hepburn were running across the cover. Tree looked up at Freddie.

He said, "*Charade?*"

24

"*Charade!*" Freddie said excitedly as Tree navigated the Ford Taurus north along I-95. "This could be the clue we're looking for."

"Interestingly, the word charade is never mentioned in the film," Tree said.

"You're the expert on these matters," Freddie said. "Tell me about the movie."

"Released in 1963, set in Paris, featuring two of the biggest stars of the time. It was directed by Stanley Donen with a nod toward Hitchcock. It's among the first in a series of romantic comedy-thrillers popular in the sixties, the best of the bunch, a classic thanks to Peter Stone's clever, witty script and, of course, the presence of Grant and Hepburn, not to mention a superb supporting cast of future stars that includes Walter Matthau, James Coburn, and George Kennedy.

"It was Grant's third-to-last movie," Tree continued. "He was nervous about the age difference between himself and Hepburn. He made sure this was pointed out in the story, enabling Hepburn to utter one of my all-time favorite lines."

"Which one is that?"

"She looks at Cary Grant and says, 'Do you know what's wrong with you? Nothing. That's what's wrong with you.' I always think of you when I hear that line."

"Flatterer," Freddie said.

"I only speak the truth," Tree replied.

"What's the movie about?"

"Like most of those films, the plot is somewhat inconsequential, an excuse for the stars to run around Paris together, looking great and saying smart things to one another. Audrey is a widow who may be the only wife in the history of the world who never asks her husband any questions—things like what he does for a living.

"After he is murdered, she discovers that he either failed to tell her or lied about everything in his life, including his real name. She is harassed and threatened by his old World War II buddies who are after the gold they arranged to steal and that has disappeared.

"Cary is a charming mystery man who changes his name as often as he changes his suit and who may or may not be on Audrey's side."

"But what's in the movie that might provide a clue for us?" Freddie asked.

"We'll have to look at it again, but offhand I can't think of anything," Tree said.

"Do they ultimately find the gold?"

"In a manner of speaking," Tree said. "It turns out the husband has used the gold to buy priceless postage stamps."

"Stamps?" Freddie sounded disappointed. "That's kind of a letdown."

"Like I said, you are not there for the plot. You're there for Audrey and Cary and Paris—oh, yes, and a great score by the brilliant Henry Mancini, lyrics by the equally brilliant Johnny Mercer. The title song is one of Dan's favorites, incidentally."

Maybe that's a clue," Freddie said.

Tree said, "Sad little serenade... Song of my heart's composing... I hear it still, I always will...Best on the bill...*Charade*..."

"What's the rest of it?"

"That's all I know," Tree said.

"That's not much of a clue." Freddie sat back, somewhat deflated, mulling over what her husband had just told her. "There must be something else," she said at length.

"Or maybe nothing," Tree said. "We'll take a look at the movie when we have a chance. But it could be charade has nothing to do with the movie."

"That's no fun," Freddie said.

"The reality of these things never is," said Tree.

"Aha," said Freddie. "The world-weary detective, down those mean streets too many times."

"That's me," Tree said.

She shoved the DVD into her shoulder bag and then reached across and took Tree's hand in hers. "Tell me what you want to do, my love."

"Todd says the police have been calling, asking where we are."

"That's not good," Freddie said.

"Todd says there's nothing much we can do if we do go back. He's right. I'm not going to be much help to Rex sitting in a jail cell."

"However, if we go on to Washington and can get to the bottom of all this, we, hopefully, won't end up in jail."

"That's what I'm thinking," Tree said.

"Then it's on to Washington?"

"Quit sounding so excited," Tree said.

25

Approaching the nation's capital after the long drive up I-95, Freddie got on the iPad searching for a place to stay. Most downtown hotels were already booked and besides, she complained, the prices they were charging for a single night were outrageous.

"Let's just get a place to stay," Tree said as they came into Washington. "This detective is dead tired."

"You're part of an investigation team that's on a budget," admonished Freddie. "We should be looking for a shabby hotel near the railway tracks with a big neon sign that blinks on and off outside our window, and a bellboy who will bring us a pint of whiskey if we slip him a few bucks."

"I don't think hotels like that exist anymore," Tree said. "And if they do, we would have to get you baby-doll pajamas before checking in."

"Baby-doll pajamas?" Freddie looked confused.

"Detectives who stay in shabby hotel rooms lit by flashing neon always encounter babes in baby-doll pajamas. If you don't believe me, just check the cover of any Shell Scott paperback."

"Shell Scott? Who is Shell Scott?"

"He was one of my favorite detectives growing up, a Los Angeles private eye created by the novelist Richard Prather," Tree said. "Shell was always encountering babes in baby-doll pajamas."

"I shudder to think what you were up to in your youth," Freddie said.

"My misspent youth, immersed in pulp fiction," Tree said.

"The Carlyle Hotel," Freddie said, eyes returned to the iPad. "They will let us in for a not-too-ridiculous price. But, unfortunately, its website specifies that no baby-doll pajamas are allowed."

"Damn," Tree said.

The Carlyle was on New Hampshire Avenue NW not far from DuPont Circle, and, it turned out, the Massachusetts Avenue address on Dan Meade's list.

By the time Tree parked in front of the hotel and turned the keys over to a parking attendant, it was growing dark. On this cool, cloudy evening in Washington, pedestrians were hurrying past on their way home from work or off to meet friends for dinner.

What a different world here, much more sophisticated than the one he inhabited most of the time, Tree mused as he lifted their single bag out of the car and handed it to a waiting bellman. This world was full of young people. The Washington power brokers were off somewhere fumbling with the levers that made their universe go uncertainly around. The worker bees were on the street, hurrying along, thin white cords protruding out of their ears, tuned into—what? Tree wondered. What was everyone listening to? NPR? Or Kanye West? Tree's money was on Kanye.

They probably wouldn't be playing rap in the Carlyle, though. The interior bespoke traditional Washington, the kind of hotel middle-aged men in three-piece suits who smoked cigars checked into when they came to town for meetings with the Eisenhower administration. Contemporary Washington was outside poring over iPhone screens for messages, wondering what you were talking about if you mentioned the Eisenhower administration.

As soon as they got to the room, Tree flopped down

onto the bed, exhausted. His eyes fluttered shut. This was better. Rest. He heard a sound and opened his eyes. Freddie came into focus.

Hovering. Impatient.

"What are you doing?"

"Just closing my eyes for a couple of minutes," Tree said defensively.

"You're going to sleep." Freddie made it sound as though falling asleep was not a good thing.

Tree struggled to sit up. "What are you suggesting, Freddie?"

"The address on Massachusetts Avenue is just around the corner. Let's take a walk over there and have a look."

"You wouldn't rather rest for a few minutes and then have a nice dinner and go there first thing in the morning?"

"I think we should at least have a look now," Freddie said. "Then we can have dinner."

Tree groaned as he struggled off the bed. "You're a slave driver," he said.

"A tough private detective like you can handle it," Freddie said.

Tree wondered.

26

Having splashed water on his face and put on the light-weight beige jacket Freddie had shoved in the carryall, Tree felt revived, taking in the evening air as they strolled along. Around them, the millennials continued to hurry, glued to their cellphones, the white wires of earbuds swinging in the evening breeze.

Freddie, ravishing in a short summer dress, took his arm—the elderly gent promenading with an eternally hot babe.

From the nighttime hustle of DuPont Circle they strolled over to Massachusetts Avenue. Elegant old buildings lined the street, housing the embassies requiring a proper address without the need for a lot of security. The buildings that were not embassies displayed impressive-looking brass plaques discreetly advertising associations Tree had never heard of.

Number 24 did not have an embassy flag above the double doors at the top of elegant stone steps. No brass plate suggested the association headquartered inside. Freddie and Tree stopped at the bottom of the steps, pretending to admire the architecture. "What do you think?" Freddie asked him.

"I'm not sure I'm thinking much of anything," Tree said.

"You should be thinking about what we do next," Freddie said.

"We go to dinner?"

"Not exactly the action plan I had in mind," Freddie said.

As they stood there, a black limousine pulled up to the

curb. A chauffeur in a black suit jumped out, went around the car to hold open the rear passenger door for a middle-aged couple, sleek and slim, dressed for the evening. They smiled their thanks and proceeded up the steps.

At the top, the man produced a white plastic card and ran it through a card swipe attached to the wall beside the door. There was an electronic buzz and the door swung open. The couple disappeared inside. The limo drove away. The street became quiet again. Tree and Freddie looked at each other: "The card," they said practically simultaneously.

"Let's think this through before we do anything," Tree said.

"What's there to think through?" Freddie replied. "We have a card. We've been wondering what it's for. Now we know."

"Do we?"

"Let's try it and see," Freddie said.

"I can't believe you're so gung-ho about this stuff."

"I'm not 'gung-ho,' as you say. But we're here, we have the card. Let's give it a try." As she spoke, Freddie was reaching into her shoulder bag. She found the card and held it up for Tree's inspection. "Shall we?"

Tree followed her up the steps. She swiped the card through the card reader. Nothing happened. Freddie tried again, slower this time. A jarring electronic buzz sounded and the door sprang ajar. Before he could stop her, Freddie pushed through. Down on the street another limo was pulling up. Tree followed Freddie inside.

A young man in evening clothes approached carrying a leather-bound book. The neatly trimmed mustache and goatee gave him a certain gravitas. "Good evening," he said.

Behind him, Tree heard the telltale electronic buzz

sound and once again the door opened. This time two men came through, burly fellows in business suits, bristling with impatience. "Omid," one of the men called. "How are you tonight?"

"Just fine, Mr. Jenkins," Omid said. "You can go right through."

"Good enough," replied the man. "I'm feeling very lucky tonight."

The two men barged past. Tree said, "I'm feeling lucky, too."

"There you go," the man said. "We'll clean them out tonight."

"You got it," Tree said, and started after the men.

Omid stopped Tree with a gentle touch on his arm. Omid's smile was guarded as he said, "We haven't seen you here before. Perhaps you could give us a name."

Tree looked at him blankly. Freddie stepped forward and said, "Dan Meade sent us."

Omid's eyes brightened noticeably. "And you have the password?"

"Of course," Freddie replied smoothly. "Charade."

Omid nodded and his smile was less guarded. "We've been waiting for you," he said. "Please go on in, have something to drink. There's food available in case you're hungry. Someone will be with you soon."

"I hope so," Freddie said. "We don't have a lot of time."

"I understand." Omid held out his hand and stepped back to allow them to pass. "This way, please," he said.

27

They entered a vast room, discreetly lit, and dominated by LCD screens you could land a helicopter on. The screens filled with ever-changing lists of statistics or with various sporting events, everything from baseball and hockey (the NHL playoffs seemed to go on forever) to horse racing, European soccer, tennis, and jai alai. A murmur of excitement rose from the crowd, eyes either on the TV screens or glued to the laptops at kiosks situated around the room. A server in a short skirt passed carrying drinks on a silver tray. She stopped to ask if Freddie and Tree wanted anything to drink. Tree demurred, but Freddie said she would like a glass of chardonnay.

"What's everyone doing here?" Freddie whispered once the server went off through the crowd.

"Sports betting," Tree said.

"Betting on what sports?"

"Everything you can imagine."

"Is this legal?"

"It wouldn't be any fun if it was," Tree said.

From the back of the room, a cheer went up, accompanied by groans. The server returned with the wine. Freddie took a sip and nodded approvingly. "They seem to know who we are."

"That's what has me worried," Tree said.

Omid appeared, smiling. "We're all set for you," he said. "Would you follow me, please?"

They had little choice but to do just that. Omid made his way to the back where the shouting had come from.

Whoever was making all the noise had quieted. Tree and Freddie trailed Omid into a corridor that led to an office.

An olive-green Aston Martin Racing suitcase held shut by two leather straps sat on a gleaming conference table, the kind ambassadors signed peace treaties on.

A sleek woman, ready for the cocktail reception following the signing of the peace treaty, rose from behind a desk at the rear of the room. The woman was striking, with a broad, horsey face. Her small dark eyes brimmed with suspicion.

Omid said, "Here they are, Estelle."

"What do we have here?" Estelle demanded. "A husband-and-wife team?"

"Hi, Estelle," Tree said.

"Where's Harry Panama?" she asked.

"Harry's not well," Tree said. "He sent us, instead."

Estelle frowned. "You mean drinking, don't you?"

"He's having some problems," Tree said.

"Booze problems." Estelle said it with a sneer.

"Irma, his wife, told us that this is the end as far as they're concerned," Freddie added.

"Good riddance," Estelle said. She looked the two of them up and down. "I hope the two of you are more reliable."

"My husband doesn't drink," said Freddie.

Estelle raised and lowered carefully plucked eyebrows. "Well, that's a first in this town."

"We've just driven from Micanopy," Tree said. "We're both tired. The sooner we get this over with the better."

"You saw Will Mickens?"

"Briefly," Tree said.

"Will's a mean son of a bitch." Estelle made it sound like a compliment. "But there's a lot of money to move around and he gets the job done. Nice if he could transport his baggy ass up to Washington every so often. We feel like we're working in the dark here."

"I'll tell him that the next time I see him," Tree said.

Estelle nodded at the suitcase. "There you go. Make sure A.T. gets this on time."

"I thought A.T. might be here tonight," Freddie said. Tree groaned inwardly, sensing immediately that was the wrong thing to say. Estelle's small black eyes once more filled with suspicion. "Why would A.T. be here?"

"Hey, we're new at this and like I say, we're tired," Tree said.

Estelle's face softened. "A.T. would never come near this place. You meet tomorrow at the Lincoln Memorial. Just like always—at least that was the way Harry always worked it."

"We got this so fast, no one told us what time tomorrow," Tree said.

"A.T. will be there about ten."

"Ten it is," Tree said. He went over and, as casually as he could, lifted the bag off the desk. It was surprisingly heavy.

Estelle glared at Omid. "Make sure you walk out with our friends."

"They don't need me," Omid said in a sullen voice.

Estelle narrowed those black eyes. "Do as you're told. Walk them out." She enunciated each word.

Omid pasted on a weak smile as he turned to Freddie and Tree. He said in a strained voice, "Please, come this way."

They followed him back into the noise and LED-fueled energy of the main room. Omid said, "Everything worked out okay?"

"Just fine," Tree said. "Thanks for your help."

"No problem," Omid said. "Stick around and have a

drink, something to eat. The place doesn't really start to jump until around midnight."

"Thanks, but we've had a long drive today," Freddie said.

Omid stopped and ushered them to one side and then stepped closer, speaking in a low voice. "Look, you're both new. I wouldn't pay too much attention to what went on back there with Estelle."

"No," Tree said.

"Changes are coming," he said. "Big changes. It's not going to be the same around here."

"You mind if I ask what the changes are going to be?" This from Freddie. Tree was amazed again at how willing she was to push at the envelope—or maybe she didn't know she was pushing at the envelope.

"Dan Meade and his group are old school," Omid said. "Their time is just about over. New generation coming in. New ideas. Fresh thinking. It's going to be exciting. Stay tuned."

"Thanks for the heads up," Tree said.

"Good seeing you," Omid said.

They went out through the door and down the steps onto the street. Another limo had stopped, disgorging more well-dressed passengers, two couples, the women dressed to kill. The latest arrivals, laughing excitedly together, sailed past Freddie and Tree, hurrying up the steps and into the house. It was nearly dark now. Neither of them said anything until they reached the bright lights and the crowds at DuPont Circle. That's when Freddie said, "What do you suppose is in that suitcase?"

"Don't worry. It's not heavy enough to be a dead body."

"Maybe it's a light dead body."

"Why would they give us a dead body?"

"Why would they give us a suitcase?"

"Because they think we are the people they were supposed to give the suitcase to."

"I just don't want to get back to the hotel and discover we have a dead body in a suitcase. We've got enough to deal with."

"What do you suggest? We open the suitcase here on the street?"

"I'm not sure what I'm suggesting," Freddie said. "I'm a little out of my depth here."

"Well, so am I," Tree said.

"Don't tell me that. You're supposed to be the hard-boiled detective."

"I'm beginning to think you're a whole lot more hard-boiled than me," Tree said. "Besides, I've now been tased. It's left me weak and uncertain."

"Have you been tased or tasered?"

"I'm not sure what difference it makes."

"If you've just been tased, you're probably okay. If you've been tasered, hey, you really are weak and uncertain."

They laughed together, and she took his arm. "What we got away with in there," she said in an awed voice.

"Amazing," he agreed.

"Let's get to the hotel," she said. "If it's a body, it's probably only part of a body."

"We can easily deal with part of a body," Tree said.

"We can deal with anything," Freddie said.

When they got back to the Carlyle, they took the elevator to their room. Tree placed the suitcase on the bed, while Freddie made sure the door was locked. Then she came and stood beside her husband. They both looked at the suitcase on the bed.

"Aston Martin Racing. That sounds expensive," Freddie said, keeping her eyes trained on the suitcase.

"It looks expensive," Tree said.

"If I was going to put a dead body in a suitcase, or part of a dead body, I wouldn't use an expensive suitcase," Freddie said.

"A cheap suitcase would do the job," Tree agreed.

"Is it locked?" Freddie asked.

Tree pressed the two locks. They snapped open. "Nope. It's not locked," he reported.

"Thanks for that," Freddie said.

Tree undid the buckles of the leather straps wrapped around the suitcase and then he stepped back.

Freddie said, "What do you think? Should we open it?"

"We've come this far," Tree said.

He moved to the bed, took a deep breath and lifted the lid.

28

There was no dead body. Just a lot of money. Thick bundles of one-hundred-dollar bills. Tree noticed that Freddie's eyes had grown very large.

"Come on," she said, somewhat breathlessly, "this can't be. This is right out of a dozen heist movies."

"I'm thinking gangster movies," Tree said. "You know, where someone gets paid off in a hotel room with a suitcase full of money."

"But those are old movies," Freddie says. "Who puts this much cash in a suitcase in this day and age?"

"People who run posh sports-betting clubs on Massachusetts Avenue."

"Someone is going to want this money," Freddie said. "Someone is going to want this money very badly."

"Yes, someone is," Tree said. "Someone like A.T. Kamala."

"Which potentially puts us in even more trouble than we're in now."

"That's a possibility," Tree said.

"What are we going to do?" Freddie asked.

"My suggestion is that we go down to the hotel restaurant and have dinner," Tree said.

"When in doubt, eat something," Freddie said.

"Exactly," Tree said.

———

The Riggsby Restaurant off the lobby was packed with

diners, the air buzzing with excitement as Freddie and Tree were seated. Once again, Tree was struck by the youth of the crowd. He was so used to sitting in restaurants full of gray-haired geezers that it came as something of a shock to discover an alternate universe filled mostly with beings who did not have white hair or lined faces and who seemed to be in pretty good shape. Who were these people, anyway? And why did they all appear to be having such a good time?

Freddie had much the same thought. "It's like all the old movers and shakers in this town are on CNN or Fox News yelling at one another. The millennials who keep the movers and shakers moving and shaking are out partying."

"I'm feeling very old," Tree said.

"Yes, but you have something all these people don't have," Freddie said.

"What's that?"

"A suitcase full of money under the bed in your room."

"I'm not so sure," Tree said. "After all, this is Washington."

Their server brought menus. Freddie ordered a glass of wine. Tree stuck with sparkling water.

"All kidding aside," Freddie said, putting her menu down and adopting a solemn expression. "What do you suppose we have gotten ourselves into?"

"I don't know much about online gambling," Tree said. "But from what I've heard, one of the problems the people behind it have is the money—what to do with all the illegal cash. We seem to have inadvertently plugged into their money-laundering supply line."

"Does that mean your friend Dan Meade, rather than being out of the bookmaking business, is still involved? The names on his list could be people he associates with in order to move illicit money."

"I doubt whether Dan is capable of dealing with anything more complicated than Johnny Mercer's song lyrics," Tree said.

"Or, he's fooling everybody, and he's capable of a lot more than just song lyrics."

The server was back to take their order: seared scallops with fava beans for Freddie; the wild striped bass for Tree.

They sat in silence for a time, taking in the cheerful cacophony of the restaurant. Freddie sipped her chardonnay. Tree strained to hear bits and pieces of the conversations going on around him. Were political secrets being traded back and forth? Was juicy gossip about what senator was sleeping with which intern being divulged? He couldn't make out a thing anyone was saying. Disappointed, he turned to Freddie, staring off.

"I can hear the machinery inside your head working overtime, Freddie. Tell me what you're thinking."

"I'm wondering how much money is in that suitcase."

"Lots."

"Hundreds of thousands, I would imagine."

"Not hard to imagine," Tree said. "Are you thinking what I'm thinking?"

"What are you thinking?"

"That we could run off with it?"

"That's not what I'm thinking." She gave him one of her disapproving looks, the one he had grown accustomed to in the past few years. "Is that what you're thinking?"

"People operating an illegal sports-betting operation just gave us a suitcase full of money. They don't know who we are or where we come from. Who's to say we can't just keep it?"

"But you wouldn't do that, would you?"

He grinned and shook his head. "No, I wouldn't."

"You're far too honest."

"I don't know about that," Tree said. "But the kind of people who gave us that suitcase aren't going to allow it to simply disappear. If we held onto it, we'd spend the rest of our lives looking over our shoulders."

"There is something else," Freddie said.

"What's that?"

"How far do you want to take this?"

"I'm not sure what you mean," Tree said.

"If you look at it a certain way, no matter what kind of shape Dan Meade's in, you've done the job he hired you for. You know what the list is about, and you know it could get him in trouble."

"We sort of know," Tree amended.

"You know he's got a problem, which is what he was worried about, right?"

"Yes, that's true."

"Then, really, there's not much more for you to do— except get into more trouble than the two of us are already in."

"There are still a lot of loose ends," Tree said.

"I hate to use the 'P' word—"

Tree groaned. "Not the 'P' word. Anything but the 'P' word."

"If there are loose ends, better that the police tie them up."

Tree closed his eyes and shook his head. "You did it. You used the 'P' word."

"What can I tell you? As ridiculous as it might sound to you, that's what most people do when they're in trouble. They call the police."

"So what are you proposing, Freddie? We go to the Washington police and tell them that I almost got blown up, found a dead body, and was handed a suitcase full of money, all because my old high school pal, Dan Meade, is suffering from dementia and is also mixed up in illegal online gambling."

Freddie made a face. "Okay, that doesn't sound good."

"What happened to the tough, gun-toting private eye who couldn't wait to confront trouble?"

"For some reason the money in the suitcase changes the equation for me. Somehow it makes everything more dangerous than it was before."

"When Sheriff Will tasered me in the parking lot, that seemed pretty dangerous."

"All the more reason why we should maybe get hold of T. Emmett Hawkins and then have a conversation with the police."

By the time their food arrived, the restaurant had quieted—young Washington headed home for a night's sleep before rising for another day of tackling the nation's problems, discovering all over again there wasn't much they could do about them, except maybe go out to another restaurant.

When they finished eating, Tree asked for the bill. The server seemed disappointed they didn't want dessert. Tree could hardly keep his eyes open.

Back in their room, Tree went into the bathroom. When he came out, Freddie had pulled the suitcase from beneath the bed and opened it up. "This isn't hundreds of thousands," she said, running her fingers over the bundles of money. "There has to be over a million dollars. It's scary."

"I'm too tired to worry about it right now," Tree said.

He lay down on the bed, closed his eyes. He heard Freddie's voice, faint now, a long way off.

29

What?

What was she saying? He wanted to tell Freddie he couldn't hear her. It was pitch black in the room. Tree could barely see his hand in front of him. He sat up in the bed, noticing a distant light. He got up and went toward it.

A lamppost illuminated a street sign: Mean Street. There was another lamppost farther along. Tree walked toward it, footsteps echoing on rain-slicked pavement. A man wearing a trench coat and a snap-brimmed fedora stood smoking a cigarette leaning against the lamppost. The smoke from his cigarette curled into the air. Beside him, on the end of a leash, was a hound dog.

"Clinton," Tree said happily as he came up to the man and the dog.

The hound perked up immediately and began to wag his tail. The man in the fedora had a rough, lived-in face, sad and world-weary. "Bogie," Tree said. "What are you doing with Clinton?"

"You got the wrong man, pal. My name's Spade."

"You're Sam Spade?"

"Should I know you?"

"No, no reason to know me. I'm just a guy looking for a dog."

"You shouldn't be out at this time of night. This is Mean Street, in case you didn't know it."

"You're out here," Tree said.

"Punks know better than to mess with me," Spade said.

"I'm searching for my dog," Tree said. "He answers to the name Clinton."

Spade produced a cynical smile. "This mutt could be your dog, I suppose. He just showed up. Apparently, he likes me."

"He's a talking dog," Tree said.

"He hasn't said a word to me. I found him wandering on the street. If you've got a talking dog, it seems like you should take better care of him."

"I know," Tree said. "There are a lot of things I should have done better."

"So you got no one to blame but yourself," Spade admonished. "Clinton and me, we're waiting for you. The way things are going, it won't be long before you join us."

Clinton rose from his haunches and padded over to Tree, lowering his head and wagging his tail harder. Tree knelt to pet him.

Spade shook his head disdainfully as he took another drag on his cigarette. "What's wrong with you, anyway? You give private eyes a bad name."

"You're right. I'm too emotional lately. Too much is happening. Too many people leaving. Too much worry that I'm next."

Spade said, "They're playing you for a sap, making you think if you do this or that, you don't do that or the other thing, you'll live forever. That's crap. Any way you cut it, you're walking toward the abyss. That's where you end up, no matter what."

Clinton cocked his head and looked up soulfully at Tree. He tickled the dog's ears. Clinton's big eyes lost their soulful look, filling with pleasure. Tree could stay here forever like this, petting his appreciative and loving dog. But there was a background noise, an electronic buzzing of some sort. It grew louder. Clinton drew away. Spade took one last drag on his cigarette and raised his head, listening to the sound.

"Looks like that's it, kid. Time to go."

"No, not yet, please."

"Sorry, kid. Everything comes to an end. You ought to know that by now."

Clinton went back to Spade. The streetlight began to dim as the electronic sound grew louder, overwhelming everything.

Tree awoke with a jerk and a loud grunt. Beside him, Freddie was turning on her side. His cellphone made sounds. He reached over and picked it up, recognizing the number on the screen. He swiped it open.

Todd Jackson said, "Tree, it's me."

"Is everything all right? Tree asked.

"I'm at the hospital. Rex has taken a turn for the worse. It's not looking good. I'm not sure where you are, and I don't want to unduly worry you, but I think you'd better get back here as soon as you can."

30

Rex was in the intensive care unit at Lee Memorial Hospital, hooked up to an array of tubes. Tree couldn't be sure, but he thought he detected a flicker of recognition when he took his old friend's hand in his. Maybe he was imagining this, as he was imagining so much these days when it came to the end of things.

"He knows you're here, Tree," Todd Jackson reassured. Standing beside Tree, Todd looked fresh even after days hanging in with his friend.

Freddie sat on the far side of the bed holding Rex's other hand. After a few moments, she got up and leaned over and kissed Rex softly on his forehead. She turned to Tree. "I'd better go home and make sure everything's all right."

"I'll drive her," Todd said. "You can spell me for a while. I'm kind of dead."

"That's fine," Tree said.

Freddie kissed Tree and then they were gone and he was alone with his oldest friend. Rex's chest moved gently up and down, the heart monitor stitching graceful green lines that gleamed in the failing light of the room. Death was close; he could feel its presence. *Doomsday is near; die all, die merrily.* Damn! Shakespeare! Just when you didn't want him.

Tree's cellphone began to vibrate. He wasn't supposed to have a cellphone with him in the intensive-care ward, but he did have it, and since he and Rex were alone, he decided to take the chance and swipe it open.

"What the hell do you think you're doing?" Dan Meade demanded angrily.

Tree didn't say anything. Dan said, "Tree, are you there?"

"I'm here, Dan."

"Where are you?"

"I'm in Fort Myers."

"What are you doing there?"

"A friend of mine is very ill. I'm back here with him."

"You weren't supposed to do that."

"What do you think I'm supposed to do?"

Dan didn't say anything. Tree said, "Dan, do you remember what you hired me for?"

"Of course, I remember," Dan erupted. "What do you take me for? A dummy? What I want to know is why you haven't produced results."

"There are a lot of things going on, Dan, things you may not know about."

"Of course, I know. Don't play games with me."

"I'm not the one playing games."

"What are you saying? That I'm somehow leading you on?"

"I think we need to sit down together and talk."

"That's not possible," Dan said curtly.

"Tell me where you are, and I can come to you."

The line went dead.

Tree sat for a few minutes, resting his hand on Rex's arm. A nurse entered the room. Tree recognized her. "Nurse Lindsay."

"I heard you were here, Mr. Callister," she said. "It's kind of weird, actually."

"Why is that?"

"To see you sitting beside a hospital bed, instead of being in it."

Tree laughed. "I've reformed, Nurse Lindsay. I stay away from situations that might get me beaten up or shot."

"Are you still a private detective?"

"Occasionally," he said.

"Oh, dear." She looked chagrined. "That might not be the best profession for you."

"You could be right," Tree said.

Lindsay checked the lines tethered to Rex and then studied the monitor. She said to Tree, "I guess I don't have to ask how you're doing."

"Concerned about my pal here," Tree said.

"We are all very concerned about Mr. Baxter, but this morning he seems to have rallied a bit." She smiled. "Maybe he's feeling better now that you're with him."

"I hope so," Tree said.

"Mr. Callister? Can I be honest with you?"

"Of course."

"Mr. Baxter has had a pretty bad heart attack. Given his age and everything, his prognosis is not good. I hope you don't mind me telling you that."

"No, no," Tree said. "I understand what you're saying."

"It's just that the nurses here see a lot of this, and we tend to be more realistic than the doctors."

Everyone wanted to be realistic, Tree thought. Everyone wanted to tell you the truth. He preferred lies. False hopes.

Out loud he said, "Thanks, Nurse Lindsay, I appreciate that. Rex is tough. Over the years I've learned not to underestimate him."

"Sure, Mr. Callister, it's always best to be positive. You never truly know how these things turn out. So let's hope for the best."

Yes, Tree thought, always hope for the best. No matter what.

Hope. Hope. *Hope...*

———————

It was late by the time he got back to Andy Rosse Lane. Freddie was curled on the sofa with a glass of wine watching the DVD of *Charade*. Audrey Hepburn, looking chic and frightened, was running along a dark Paris street.

She turned off the television and sat up. "Do you want something to eat?"

"I'm not hungry, thanks." He bent to kiss her. "Any clues?"

"Don't be smart," Freddie retorted.

"We know what charade is—the password that got us into that Washington sports-betting club."

"Yes, but it could be something else, as well."

"You just want to watch Cary Grant and Audrey Hepburn again," Tree said.

"There are worse fates," said Freddie. "How is Rex doing?"

"Resting quietly, as they say. The nurses thought he was better."

"That's good, isn't it?"

"Yes, but he isn't out of danger yet," Tree said. "Nurse Lindsay was there, warning that given Rex's age, we should not expect too much."

"Oh, dear," Freddie said.

"I feel sick—and guilty," Tree said. "I should have been here earlier."

"But you're here now," Freddie said. "That's what counts."

"Yes," Tree said, distractedly. "We are here now."

"Unfortunately, we are here with a suitcase full of money that we don't know what to do with."

"Dan Meade called," Tree said.

"You're kidding. What did he say?"

"Not a whole lot."

"What did you say?"

"I said we should meet and talk."

"And he said?"

"He hung up."

"So what do you want to do?"

Tree shook his head. "Right now, all I can think of is Rex."

"Okay," Freddie said.

"Tell me about the movie," Tree said, sinking down beside Freddie. "Did you see anything that might help us?"

"Audrey's husband has been thrown from a moving train," Freddie said. "She discovers he's not who he says he is." She gave him a look. "I've got my eye on you."

"You don't think I am who I say I am?" Tree said.

"Sometimes I wonder," Freddie replied. "Anyway, when Audrey returns to the kind of gorgeous Paris apartment you only see in the movies, she finds it empty. Before he died, her husband sold everything—furniture, clothes, everything. Makes me wonder how she is able to run around Paris in all those Givenchy outfits. But then *Charade* is not a movie you watch for its innate logic."

"It's Paris," Tree said. "It's Cary. It's Audrey. A celebration of old guys who are still irresistible to young women."

"Yes, Cary is old enough to be Audrey's father, but never mind. There's lots of clever dialogue, and everyone thinks Audrey has her husband's money when she hasn't a clue where it is, and Cary turns out not to be who he claims he is either, and there are names, lots of names. Cary has about four of them before the movie is over."

"It all comes down to those stamps, doesn't it?"

"That's right," Freddie said. "It turns out Audrey's husband used the money to buy the world's rarest stamps and then put them on an envelope no one notices until the end of the movie. It is not explained, incidentally, how he would have gotten hold of the world's rarest stamps, paid for them with stolen money, without attracting attention."

"Details, details," Tree said.

"Maybe we should be looking for rare stamps."

"Except we have a suitcase full of money."

"That you don't want to talk about tonight."

"I can barely keep my eyes open," Tree said.

Freddie said, "All of which is to say I'm doubtful that *Charade* is going to help us much."

"Unless answers are hiding in plain sight—like those stamps."

"I still want to know how Audrey got her hands on all those Givenchy outfits," Freddie said.

By the time she finished that sentence, Tree was snoring softly beside her, his head thrown back against the sofa.

On the big screen, Audrey Hepburn's eyes had grown very large as she hid behind a pillar trying to decide if Cary Grant or Walter Matthau could be trusted.

Her money was on Cary Grant, Freddie decided. You could always trust Cary Grant, no matter what.

Tree issued a gentle snore.

31

Rex's condition had not changed overnight, according to the nurses on duty when Tree got to the hospital the next morning. He sat with his friend. Every so often Rex's eyes fluttered open, and Rex offered Tree a wan smile. A moment later, they closed again and Rex slept.

After a couple of hours, Tree took a deep breath, steeled himself for what was to come, and poked out a number he knew only too well.

"I've been looking for you," said Sanibel Island detective Cee Jay Boone when she came on the phone.

"Oh?" Tree said in the noncommittal voice he made sure he used when talking to a police officer.

"Don't tell me you don't know," Cee Jay said.

"I don't know anything," Tree said.

"Actually, to be accurate, not me so much as the Savannah police."

"Why would the Savannah police want to talk to me?"

"It has something to do with a private jet that exploded on the runway at the Savannah airport."

"I didn't do it," Tree said.

"Ha, ha," Cee Jay said without mirth. "Tree, this is serious. You should know by now that you can't just disappear the way you seem to have disappeared lately."

"I haven't disappeared. I've been traveling out of state."

"To Savannah," Cee Jay said.

"Among other places," Tree said.

"If you don't know anything about anything, why are you calling me?" Cee Jay sounded exasperated.

"It's been a while since we talked," Tree said. "I thought I'd phone and see how you're doing."

"I don't have time for this. I get a headache talking to you."

"I'm sorry about that," Tree said.

"How is Rex?" Her voice had softened.

"Better," Tree said. "I'm with him now."

"I hope he's going to be all right," Cee Jay said. "He's a nice guy, although his choice of playmates leaves something to be desired."

"He would agree with you," Tree said.

"So you're staying put?"

"Where would I go?"

She let out a sigh and then said, "Let me talk to the Savannah police. I'll find out how they want to proceed and then get back to you."

"It's always good to talk to you, Cee Jay."

"No it isn't, Tree. Every time I talk to you, it means a truckload of trouble is headed down the road toward me, and you're behind the wheel."

Then she was gone. Everyone was hanging up on him lately.

Rex stirred on the bed. Tree adjusted the covers. A nurse entered, smiled frostily at Tree, and then addressed Rex in a loud voice, "How are you doing this morning, Mr. Baxter?"

Rex did not respond.

"I don't think he's going to say anything," Tree said.

The nurse gave him another frosty smile, checked Rex's pulse, and then swished silently away.

Tree made another phone call.

When he came on the line, T. Emmett Hawkins said, "Not more trouble."

"Maybe I'm not in any trouble," Tree said. "Maybe I'm just calling to say hello."

"Nobody calls me just to say hello, least of all you. What have you done now?"

"The Savannah police want to talk to me in connection with a plane that blew up on the tarmac there."

"This is the jet belonging to Dandy Dan Meade I read about?" Hawkins said.

"That's the one," Tree said.

"Obviously, you weren't on the plane," Hawkins said.

"I was just about to get on when it exploded."

"What were you doing with Dan Meade?"

"Dan is a client. I was there in connection with a case. That's how I ended up in Micanopy with our friend Sheriff Will Mickens."

"A varmint if there ever was one," Hawkins said. "I hate to bring this up because it doesn't seem to make much difference, but I thought you retired."

"I'm back to work—sort of," Tree said. "Dan wanted me to look into something for him."

"Which brought you to the attention of the police,"

"Apparently," Tree said.

Hawkins was silent, as though taking time to digest this information. Then he said, "So after the jet exploded, what did you do?"

"I left."

"And why would you do that?"

"I was afraid whoever blew up the plane was after Dan," Tree said. "I thought I'd better get to him as quickly as possible."

"I suppose I don't have to tell you that leaving the scene like that was not in your best interest," Hawkins said.

"Then when I got to Dan's place in Savannah, there was a dead body."

A longer silence this time. "Dan Meade?" Hawkins ventured.

"His assistant, a woman named Prudence Colt."

"What about Dan?"

"There was no sign of him," Tree said.

"Can I assume you did not call the police?"

"That's right," Tree said.

Tree heard a sharp intake of breath before Hawkins said, "You realize that leaving the scene of a murder is also a mistake."

"I believed I had to find Dan, that if I waited around for the police to show, there would be all sorts of questions and it would be too late to save Dan."

"Have you subsequently found him?"

"No, but he's called me a couple of times, so I know he's still alive—in hiding, I believe, but alive."

"What does he say about all this?"

"Not much. Dan is suffering from CTE. I'm not certain how aware he is of any of this."

Hawkins issued another deep sigh. "All right, leave it with me. At some point you're going to have to go into police headquarters and provide a statement. Make sure I'm there when you do."

"Thanks, Emmett, I appreciate this."

"One more thing while I've got you on the phone."

"Yes?"

"I should tell you that you are not in trouble."

"Glad to hear it."

"You are in a *lot* of trouble."

The third person Tree had talked to that morning then hung up on him. Something of a record, he thought.

Tree sat with Rex for another hour before his phone rang again. A voice said, "Mr. W. Tremain Callister?"

Whenever anyone used his full name, Tree knew it was trouble. He swallowed a couple of times before he said, "Yes? Who's this?"

"Mr. Callister, this is Dan Meade's wife calling."

"I didn't know Dan had a wife," Tree said.

"In fact, he's got several of them," the caller said. "I'm the latest. My name's Charade. Charade Meade."

32

Two women were waiting for Tree when he got to his office at the Chamber of Commerce Visitors Center. One of the women, tall and lanky in an ankle-length summer dress done in black and white patterns, straw-colored hair falling to bare shoulders, sat reading a copy of the *Island Sun*.

The other woman occupied herself studying the swordfish-catching, bikini-clad model on the wall over Tree's desk. The second woman had short-cropped gray hair and wore a stripped top over a pair of white culottes.

The lanky woman looked up from her newspaper as Tree entered while the woman with the short-cropped hair ended her study of the photograph and said, "That's a ridiculous picture."

Tree looked at her.

"I mean, would anyone wear a skimpy bikini to catch a swordfish?"

"It's not the swordfish she's after," the lanky woman said, putting the *Island Sun* to one side. "It's the guy taking the picture."

"It doesn't make sense," the woman with the short-cropped hair said, faintly irritated. She turned her attention to Tree. "You're a detective," she said accusingly. "What are you doing with a picture like that?"

"It was hanging on the wall when I moved in," Tree explained.

"What?" said the woman with the short-cropped hair. "You've been too busy solving cases here on Sanibel Island to change it?" She made it sound as though he hadn't been busy at all.

"I believe it has more to do with laziness," Tree said, closing the door and moving toward his desk. "Also, I've come to the conclusion that that woman and myself are kindred spirits. We both get into unexpected trouble without being dressed properly for it."

The tall, lanky woman said, "You think we're trouble?"

"Are you?" retorted Tree.

The woman with the short-cropped hair addressed the tall, lanky woman. "You see? I told you he was a smart detective."

"Yes, you did," agreed the tall, lanky woman. She gave Tree a dazzling smile. "And not unattractive for an older man."

Tree looked at the two women and said, "I assume one of you is Charade Meade."

"There you go," pronounced the woman with the short-cropped hair. "Our man also possesses great deductive skills."

"A regular Sherlock Holmes," the tall, lanky woman said. She gave Tree another dazzling smile. "I'm Charade."

"As in the word-guessing game?" Tree asked.

"As in the movie starring Cary Grant and Audrey Hepburn," said Charade. "My mother said it was the first movie she and my father ever saw together."

"Your father was a son of a bitch," the woman with the short-cropped hair said.

"That's another story," said Charade Meade.

"Also, the word *charade* is never mentioned," the woman with the short-cropped hair said, sounding irritable again. "I don't understand how it's the title of the movie."

Charade rolled lovely blue eyes. "This is an ongoing discussion," she said.

Tree trained his gaze on the woman with the short-cropped hair. "You haven't told me your name."

"I'm glad you can finally pull your eyes away from the buxom blond in the room," she said.

Charade demonstrated how a catty smile would look on her as she said, "He hasn't moved his eyes."

The woman with the short-cropped hair frowned and said, "I'm the other Meade. Doris. Doris Meade. Dumped Doris as Charade calls me during moments of frustration."

"Frequent moments of frustration," Charade added.

"You said it, not me," Doris said.

"Doris was married to Dan before I was," Charade explained.

"I was the second Mrs. Meade," Doris said.

"Dan left Doris for me," Charade said.

"Except I got my revenge, didn't I?" chimed in Doris.

"I left Dan for Doris," Charade said.

"The blond bombshell and the old broad with gray hair," Doris said. "Who would have believed it?"

"I don't think Dan believes it," Charade said.

"I doubt Dan realizes what's happened," Doris said.

Charade looked at Tree. "Dan has dementia, you see."

"We believe it's Alzheimer's," said Doris.

"Although we can't be sure," added Charade.

"As a result of his worsening condition, Charade and I have found it necessary to take over Dan's business affairs."

"What kind of business is that?" Tree asked.

Charade Meade looked surprised. "You don't know?"

"I suppose I know what I've read," Tree said, choosing his words carefully, not quite certain what they knew or didn't know.

Doris said, "Then you understand Dan has—or had—interests in online gambling."

"Yes," Tree said.

"We have now taken control of those interests," Charade said. "And let me tell you, we have our work cut out for us."

"Okay, but I'm not quite certain where I fit into this," Tree said.

"You and Dan being high school pals," Doris said, as though being high school pals made all the sense in the world.

"During his few lucid moments, Dan spoke highly of you," Charade said. "That's how we learned you are now a private detective here in South Florida."

"Dan kept saying he wanted to hire you," Doris said. "But of course nothing ever came of it."

"No," Tree said.

"But we now have need of the services of a discreet private investigator," Charade said.

"We put the stress on that word discreet," Charade added.

Charade leaned forward producing one of the smiles with which she lured men to their doom. "Let's say you are discreet, Mr. Callister. But how good are you?"

Tree cleared his throat and said, "Please call me Tree."

"What about it, Tree?" Doris said. She did not lean forward. She did not smile.

"What is it you need me to do?"

Charade sat back and took on a businesslike demeanor. "Part of Dan's enterprise involves cash collections. The other night in Washington, a couple showed up. The staff for some reason believed the couple was authorized to make a pickup."

"In fairness to the Washington team, this couple did appear legitimate," Doris added. "They had an entry card and they even had the correct password. There was no reason not to give them the money."

"Whatever the reasons," Charade went on in her businesslike voice, "the money was handed over to these people and it shouldn't have been."

"They were supposed to turn over the money the next morning to an associate, but they never showed up," Doris said.

"This couple stole the money," Charade said.

Tree discovered, as he usually did in these circumstances, that he was having trouble swallowing. "How much did they take?"

"One million, five hundred thousand dollars," Charade said.

"In cash," added Doris.

"What about surveillance video?" Tree's words sounded strained coming out of his mouth.

"In this business, in those places, surveillance video is not an option," Charade said. "Although we are convinced we are involved in a legal enterprise, the authorities aren't always quite so certain."

"The couple that took this money," Tree said.

"What about them?" Doris said.

"You have no sense at all as to who these people are?"

"If we knew who they were, we'd go after them." Doris made it sound as though any fool should know this.

Charade was leaning forward again. The dazzling smile was back. "That's where you come in, Tree."

Doris still wasn't smiling. "We want you to find the couple and get our money back."

Tree was trying to think fast, to come up with something that would make sense. He couldn't think of anything. The women stared at him. Charade finally said, "You're not saying anything."

"I'm not sure what to say," Tree answered truthfully.

"Say that you'll find our money and return it to us," Doris suggested.

"Yes, that's one way of answering," Tree agreed.

"Is there any other way?" Charade was no longer producing enticing smiles.

"There is this: I don't know how I'm going to get your money back for you," Tree finally offered. "This happened in Washington, D.C. I am on Sanibel Island."

"We're aware of that," Doris said. "We still believe you're the man for the job."

"Also, Dan vouches for you," Charade added. "Because he knows you so well, we can rely on you for—well, there's that word again—discretion."

"Here's another reason to take the job," Doris said. She reached into a large soft leather bag on the floor beside her chair and withdrew a bulging manila envelope. She set the envelope on the desk in front of Tree.

"What's that?" he asked.

"That's thirty thousand dollars in cash," Doris said. "We don't know what you charge or what your expenses will be, but that should get you started. If you need more, let us know."

Tree kept his eyes on the envelope.

"But I have to have something to go on," he said. The words were out of his mouth before he realized he was arguing for more information that would lead to the person responsible for the disappearance of more than a million dollars—him.

"We want you to fly up to Washington, talk to our people, see what you can learn about the robbers' identities and go from there," Charade said.

"Frankly, we suspect some sort of inside job," Doris said. "How else would they get information about the club?"

Charade focused those blue eyes on Tree, eyes full of inviting warmth. "I think Tree can get us what we need. What about it, Tree? Can you do it?"

Vaguely in the background, Tree could hear Doris say, "Charade, are you working overtime to make me jealous? Or is it happening accidentally?"

Charade kept her eyes on Tree. "What about it, Tree?"

"Tree, we need an answer," Doris, impatient. "Are you going to pick up that money and help us out? What's it going to be?"

Tree stared at the envelope.

33

What could I say?" Tree said after he joined Freddie in Rex's room and told her about his encounter with the two Meades.

"How about 'no'?" Freddie said.

"If I said no, then they would have hired someone else who might trace the money back to us," Tree said.

"Which is why we should get rid of the money," Freddie said.

"How do you propose we do that?"

"Turn it over to the authorities."

They were speaking in low voices seated together at Rex's bedside. He lay peacefully as Freddie shook her head and looked pained. "I can't believe this is happening," she said.

"How do you think I feel?" Tree said.

"So if we don't turn the money over to the police, what do we do?"

Tree didn't answer immediately. Then he said, "They want me to go to Washington and talk to their people."

"They want you to go?"

"That's right," Tree answered

"And talk to the people who gave us the money in the first place."

"Yes."

"The people who will recognize us as soon as we walk in the door."

"They could."

Freddie said, "That's going to slightly complicate things, don't you think?"

"No doubt about it."

"Also," Freddie continued, "earlier you said 'me' as opposed to 'us.'"

"I did say that."

"I don't like it," Freddie said.

"I understand, but I'd feel a lot better if you weren't involved," Tree said.

"It's too late for that kind of male thinking," Freddie said. "I'm already involved."

"It's not male thinking," Tree insisted. "It's I-don't-want-my-wife-hurt thinking."

"Here's what I suggest," Freddie said. "We go to Washington, spend some time, then come back and turn over the money to the Meade ladies. Brilliant detective work. You were able to find the cash and return it to its rightful owners. Problem solved—and no one gets hurt, least of all the two of us."

"I'm not sure it's going to be that easy," Tree said.

"Then let's have a better idea."

Instead of answering, Tree turned his gaze on Rex. "Also, there's this guy. He's not better yet, and I don't want to leave him."

"Then let me go up there," Freddie said.

"No way," said Tree adamantly. "If anything happened to you I'd never forgive myself."

"I like that," Freddie said. "A lifetime of guilt."

"I'm not letting you do this alone."

"Then we do this together. All for one. One for all."

"We're not the Three Musketeers," Tree said.

"Two," Freddie said. "The two of us. A team. Sticking together through hell or high water."

They were interrupted by the arrival of Sanibel detectives Cee Jay Boone and Owen Markfield. Neither of them looked happy.

"We've been looking for the two of you," Cee Jay said.

"Did T. Emmett Hawkins call you?" Tree asked.

"We're not here to talk to your lawyer, Callister," Owen Markfield said. "We've been trying to reach you."

"I've been right here or at the office," Tree said. "Not hard to find."

Freddie stood to face the two detectives. "I'm sure Tree would be glad to cooperate with you in any way he can." She turned to her husband. "Wouldn't you, darling?"

"Absolutely," Tree said.

"That would be a first," Markfield said.

"Let's go down to the lobby where we can talk more comfortably," Freddie said.

"Why don't we put the cuffs on the two of you and haul you down to police headquarters?" Markfield snarled.

"All right," Cee Jay said, stepping forward, "I don't think that's going to be necessary. Let's all meet in the lobby and see if we can't get the answers we need." She looked at Tree. "But I'll tell you, Tree, if we don't get answers, then it is handcuffs and a ride to police headquarters."

"Just don't let Owen at me with his rubber hose," Tree said.

Markfield made an ugly noise deep in his throat.

34

They sat uncomfortably on the strap-back chairs in the hospital's vast atrium, a setting that encouraged, if not silence, certainly the respectful lowering of voices.

Just as well, Tree thought, as he perched nose-to-nose with his arch-nemesis, Owen Markfield. With his exquisitely coiffed blond hair, his sun-burnished square jaw, his gray-suede Ugg loafers, the loose-fitting Tommy Bahama shirt over white Ralph Lauren jeans, Owen was camera-ready for his close-up in a TV cop series set in South Florida. Pity no one had discovered Markfield and made him a star, thus saving Tree from the detective's vengeful clutches. Past transgressions had made Markfield a determined enemy.

Tree was less certain about Cee Jay Boone, the fortyish no-nonsense African-American woman he might consider an ally, except that when they first met she tried to kill him—something she had always denied. The district attorney's office had failed to make a case, Cee Jay returned to duty, and Tree had had to deal with her ever since.

Despite their history, Tree felt better with her sitting next to Markfield. She was no friend, but these days she was not an enemy, either.

Cee Jay led the questioning, not wasting any time getting to the point: "We're looking for your friend, Dan Meade. Where is he, Tree?"

"First of all, Dan Meade's not a friend," Tree said.

"I understand you went to high school together in Chicago."

"I knew him in high school, but as he was a star football player, and very popular, so did everyone else."

Tree noticed Freddie, the great stone face, inscrutable, perfect for a poker game—or a police interrogation.

"So what are you saying, Callister? You don't know where he is?" Tree noticed that the veins stood out on Markfield's tanned neck when he spoke.

"That's what I'm saying."

Cee Jay said in a less accusatory voice, "Tree, the Savannah police have been looking at surveillance recordings of Dan Meade's private jet when it blew up on the tarmac."

"Yes," Tree said.

"Someone can be seen driving away from the airport in a Lincoln registered to Mr. Meade. Later, that car was found near a residence owned by Mr. Meade in the old part of Savannah. Inside the residence, police found the body of Mr. Meade's assistant, a woman named Prudence Colt. Do you know anything about any of this?"

"Should I?"

Markfield gave Tree a hard, accusatory look, one that he was all too used to receiving from the detective. "It's you in that surveillance footage, Callister. You're the one driving away from the airport."

"That's quite an accusation," Tree said.

"But is it you?" Cee Jay asked.

"I would have to refer you to my lawyer about that," Tree said.

"What the hell is that supposed to mean?" Markfield demanded.

"It means Tree should not be answering these sorts of questions without a lawyer present," Freddie said calmly.

Cee Jay threw Markfield a look before she addressed Tree. "Are you saying you won't answer the question?"

Freddie once again interjected, this time in a more formal voice: "I'm advising my husband not to say any more until we've had a chance to consult with his lawyer. I believe you are familiar with T. Emmett Hawkins."

"We should haul your ass in," Markfield snarled at Tree. Freddie was on her feet. "Come on, Tree. Let's go."

Tree got to his feet. Like a shot, Markfield was out of his seat, knocking it over. "You're not going anywhere," he said to Tree.

"Detective Markfield," Cee Jay said quietly. "That's enough." She was on her feet as well, addressing Tree. "You should know that Dan Meade is wanted in connection with the explosion that destroyed his private jet."

Tree looked at her in amazement. "You think he blew up his own plane?"

"The Savannah police also want him in connection with the death of Prudence Colt," Cee Jay said.

"He blew up his plane and then killed his assistant?" Tree had no trouble adding a note of incredulity to his voice.

"All I know is that the Savannah police have a warrant for him," Cee Jay said.

"According to his wife, he's suffering from dementia," Tree said. "I don't see how he'd be capable of blowing anything up."

Markfield looked at him curiously. "Dementia? Are you kidding? Dan Meade isn't suffering from dementia—at least not as far as the Savannah police are concerned."

"I think we're finished here, Detective Markfield," Cee Jay interjected pointedly. To Tree she said, "We will be in touch."

"You bet we will," Markfield said.

Freddie stepped forward to give Markfield a fierce look. "Don't you ever get tired of threatening my husband?"

"Never," replied Markfield.

Cee Jay pulled Markfield away. Then she stopped and turned to Tree. "I don't know what you're up to, Tree, or how you're involved in this. But it's obvious someone is providing you with very inaccurate information."

"Such as?" Tree said.

"Like Detective Markfield said, we have no indication this suspect is suffering from anything that could be described as dementia. Also, as far as his wife is concerned..."

"What about her?"

"Dan Meade's wife died of cancer five years ago."

35

The house at Andy Rosse Lane had been ransacked. Someone had jimmied open the rear door. The burglar alarm might have stopped the intruders—that is, if Tree had remembered to set it.

Freddie and Tree looked at one another. Tree said, "Where did you hide the money?"

Freddie swallowed before she said, "Under the bed."

"Under the bed?" Tree, trying to keep the note of astonishment out of his voice—failing.

"Where else would you hide a suitcase full of money—knowing that my husband would set the alarm before we went out?"

Tree did not have a ready answer for that question.

Their bedroom had been turned upside down. The suitcase was not under the bed. "Maybe," Freddie conceded, "that was not the best place to hide the money."

"Especially when I forget to set the alarm," Tree added.

"The question is, who would have known we even had the money?" Freddie said.

"That's a very good question," Tree agreed. "I wish I had the answer."

"Well, it's gone and the place is a mess," Freddie said. "What do we do now? Call the police?"

"And tell them someone broke in here and stole a suitcase containing one-and-a-half million dollars that we stole from a betting club in Washington?"

"We didn't steal it, and there wasn't a million dollars in the suitcase."

"How do you know that?" Tree asked.

"I counted it, of course," Freddie said. "There was only seven hundred and fifty thousand."

"The Meade ladies said one million five hundred thousand."

"You mean the two women who told you they were married to Meade and weren't? They are probably lying. Either that or someone is lying to them."

They spent the next hour or so getting the house more or less in shape before giving up and retreating downstairs to the rear terrace, Freddie with her chardonnay, Tree with his Diet Coke. They listened to the clamor from the nearby Mucky Duck, the evening ritual of tourist excitement over the sun going down.

"I don't know why I don't just sit here for the rest of my life, listening to happy tourists at the Mucky Duck, watching the sunset, sipping Diet Coke and contemplating my misspent life."

"Contemplate your misspent life after we go to Washington," Freddie said.

Tree gave her a surprised look. "What's the point?" he said. "We don't have the money."

"Your friends the Meades—if that's who they are—hired you to find the money," Freddie reminded him.

"I'll just tell them I've changed my mind," Tree said. "My best friend is very sick, and right now I can't go anywhere."

"That way nothing is resolved," Freddie said. "You've still got problems with the police, with the Meade women, and your friend Dan remains missing—and you never really solve the mystery."

"Maybe there is no solving of this mystery—or any mystery for that matter. Maybe there's just sitting on this terrace watching the sun set."

"What are you going to do with yourself after the sun goes down?"

"I visit Rex who may be dying. I hold his hand and despair over the fragility of life and how everyone I love is leaving."

"You haven't lost me," Freddie said.

Tree smiled and said, "That is the one thing that keeps me going."

"You could be right about the mystery," Freddie said. "Maybe we can't solve it, but I'd like to try."

"I'm tired of mysteries," Tree said. "I want life to be simple, uncomplicated, and everyone lives happily forever."

"Good luck with that," Freddie said. She rose to her feet. "Let's do it this way. We see how Rex is doing and then decide what we're going to do next."

"Why I love you," Tree said. "One of the many reasons."

"I know you love me," Freddie said. She came and bent over him. "The question that must be asked…"

"Yes?"

"*Why* do I love you?"

Freddie softened the question with a kiss on Tree's mouth.

36

Rex Baxter said, "Thanks for inviting me to your birthday party, Frank."

Tree Callister, seated beside Rex's bed, recovered from his shock at suddenly hearing his friend speak, before leaning forward and saying, "What?"

"It's a hell of a party, Frank," Rex mumbled. His eyes fluttered as he spoke, as though he was trying to pry them open. "Did I tell you? I was sitting beside this beautiful actress. Tiny but so sexy. Her name is Salma Hayek, Frank. She's gorgeous."

Rex's eyes opened and he looked at Tree. "I should have run off with Salma," he said. "I wonder if she would have had anything to do with me."

"Here I thought you were dying," Tree said. "Turns out you were just dreaming of Salma Hayek."

"Frank Sinatra's eightieth birthday party at the Shrine Auditorium. Frank invited me. At least I think it was Frank. Anyway, I ended up there at the Shrine."

"With Salma Hayek."

"I wonder if she would have married me if I asked her."

"How could she resist?"

"She might have saved me a lot of pain and trouble—or caused me a whole lot more pain and trouble. Hard to say how it would have played out."

"The one that got away," Tree said.

"It was a weird night. Frank looked great, but his mind was going. Bob Dylan was there. What the hell was Dylan doing there? Louis Jourdan, too. Now he really did look great. Like he just walked off the set of *Gigi*." Rex was silent for a moment. His eyes closed.

Tree said, "Rex?"

His friend's eyes popped open. "The party's over, I guess. Probably Salma left with someone else. Damn shame. Do you mind if I ask you where I am?"

"You are at Lee Memorial."

"I'm not in heaven with Salma Hayek?"

"Not yet," Tree said.

"That's a relief, I suppose."

"How are you feeling?"

"Like I've been asleep for a long time. I don't suppose there's any water."

Tree got him ice water and then lifted up his friend's head so that he could suck out of a straw. "That's better," he said, lying his head back down again.

Tree's cellphone rang. He looked at the read-out, didn't recognize the number. "You'd better take that," Rex said in a whispery voice. "You being a world-famous detective and all."

Tree swiped his phone open and a voice said, "You're not still in town, are you?"

Tree said, "Who's this?"

"This is your employer," the voice said. "Who do you think it is?"

"Doris?"

"Charade. Charade Meade. The cute wife who kept making eyes at you."

"Yes," Tree said.

"Why aren't you in Washington?"

"I've got a few things to tie up here first."

"*Things?*" There was disbelief in Charade's voice. "What *things?*"

"I have done some poking around," Tree said.

"Funny," Charade said. "I don't remember asking you to 'poke' around. I do remember *hiring* you to find our money."

"My initial investigation reveals that Dan Meade's wife died five years ago."

That brought silence on the other end of the line. Tree said, "Are you there?"

"Yes, of course, I'm here." Charade sounded peeved. "I'm just trying to decide whether you are a total moron or simply off on the wrong investigative foot."

"What does that mean?"

"It means Dan's first wife died five years ago. He married Doris three years ago. A year later, he met me and dumped Doris. Then I met Doris and dumped Dan."

"Okay, but that's not the information I received."

"Then the information you received is wrong," Charade pronounced. "Besides, your job is not to investigate Dan's marital history. Your job, as I keep repeating, is to find that money. Please, stop this other nonsense and get to work."

Then she hung up.

Tree looked at Rex. His eyes were closed. He was breathing gently, his chest moving up and down.

Asleep.

Tree's cellphone sounded again. It was Freddie this time. "I'm outside in the car," she said.

"Okay, I'll come out. Rex is awake."

"How is he?"

"Talking about Frank Sinatra's eightieth birthday party. I think he's going to survive."

"Get out here," Freddie said.

Freddie had pulled up to the front entrance in her Mercedes. Somehow she had been able to get it back from the Cotton Sail. There were companies that would do this, she discovered, pick up your car and drive it anywhere.

When he got in the car, she saw that she was made up and wearing a bright summer dress. He took note of the carryall in the backseat. "What's up?"

"I've been thinking," Freddie said.

"About what?"

"About who would have known we had the money."

"And?"

"I think I know. But in order to be sure, we have to drive back to Washington."

"How did you manage to figure this out?" Tree asked.

"I'm not certain I have," Freddie said. "For now, let's call it a woman's intuition."

"I haven't heard that for a while," Tree said. "Besides, I thought we weren't going to Washington."

"If Rex didn't regain consciousness. He's regained consciousness, so now we can go."

Freddie somehow made it all sound reasonable.

"I don't remember agreeing to anything like that," Tree said.

"That's because you're getting old and your memory may be fading."

"I just got a call from an unhappy Charade Meade."

"What did she say?"

"She said she was the wife making eyes at me."

"Except she's not a wife, is she?"

"She's sticking to her story—she's Dan's wife. So is Doris."

"Right now, it doesn't make much difference," Freddie said.

"She's wondering why I'm not out finding her money."

"All the more reason to go to Washington," Freddie said. "She wants her money. That's where it is."

37

Rain pelted down, obscuring the view of Massachusetts Avenue. Grim passersby in rain gear, huddled beneath umbrellas, faded in and out of misty view as Freddie and Tree sat in their rented Buick parked not far from the sports-betting club they previously visited.

They had flown into Washington that morning, rented a car at the airport, and then made their way into town through traffic snarled by rain.

It continued to rain, steaming the windows so that Tree could barely see the stone steps of the club.

"I'm not sure this is going to work." Tree said.

"What is it you're not sure about?" said Freddie.

"This. Sitting out here on the street, hoping against hope he's going to come along."

"Being a private detective requires patience," Freddie said.

"Who told you that?"

"A private detective I know," Freddie said.

"Because you were so impatient doing this sort of thing," Tree said.

"That was before I got cred on the mean streets of America."

"Right," Tree said. "I forgot."

Freddie sat up abruptly, then leaned forward, wiping at the windshield, trying to get a clearer view of the street.

"Do you see something?"

Without answering, Freddie reached into the bag beside her on the floor and pulled out a Glock automatic. Tree's eyes widened when he saw it.

"What's that?"

"What's it look like?" she said. "It's a gun."

"I understand that, but where did you get it?"

"I packed it in our checked luggage," Freddie said.

"You can do that?"

"You certainly can," said Freddie. "Haven't you read the Constitution? All decent, law-abiding citizens can pack guns in their luggage when they're flying."

"I can't believe you brought the gun," Tree said.

"Let's just say that although I am not in favor of guns, I thought it might be wise to have one—if needed. Here." She handed him the Glock.

"What am I supposed to do with this?"

"Stick it under your jacket just in case," she said.

"Just in case of what?"

"Just in case it's needed," Freddie said opening the driver's-side door. "Come on. We're going to miss him."

"Miss who?"

But Freddie was already out of the car. Tree jammed the gun in his belt and opened the door and got out on the street. It was gray and miserable, the rain continuing to come down. Freddie was already confronting a young man with black hair wearing a long blue trench coat. It was Omid, the doorman from the betting club.

Freddie said, "Hi, Omid, remember me?"

Omid looked startled.

Freddie continued: "You gave us some money a week ago. Then you realized you'd made a mistake, figured out who we were, and followed us back to Sanibel. I don't imagine you acted alone. Or did you? Anyway, you waited until we left the house and then broke in, found the suitcase with the money, and stole it."

"I did not steal anything." Omid had recovered his voice along with a rain-streaked scowl.

"If you returned it to your employer—Estelle?—then you're right, you didn't steal it. So let's go ask her, shall we?"

The scowl on Omid's face deepened. "I don't know what you are talking about," he said. "You are a crazy woman."

"Charade Meade doesn't think so," Freddie said. "She's hired me and my husband to get her money back."

At the mention of Charade's name, the scowl disappeared. Omid's face went blank.

"Let's get in the car, out of the rain so we can talk," Freddie said in her best let's-solve-this-problem-together voice.

"I am not going anywhere with you," Omid said.

"Tree," Freddie said, keeping her eyes on Omid. "Show him why he should get in the car."

"What?" Tree said.

Freddie made a jabbing motion with her hand. "What you've got. Show him what you've got."

Tree looked confused. "What have I got?"

Freddie looked annoyed and made more jabbing motions with her hand. "You know—that—"

"You mean the gun," Tree said.

"Yes," Freddie said. "The *gun*."

Tree addressed Omid. "Get in the car, Omid. I've got a gun."

"Yeah, sure," Omid said dubiously. "Old white guy on a Washington street with a gun. Give me a break."

Tree showed him the Glock. Omid didn't look quite so dubious. Freddie said, "We just want to talk, Omid. It's all right. Get in the car."

Freddie opened the rear passenger door for him. Omid hesitated, made a face like he wasn't going to do as he was told, but then he appeared to deflate a bit and ducked into the car.

Freddie turned to Tree. "You slide in beside him, Tree."

Then Freddie got into the front passenger seat.

Once Tree was inside and the doors closed, Freddie twisted around to face Omid and said, "Listen to me carefully, Omid. We know you've got the money. The good news for you is that right now, no one else does."

"You're out of your mind," Omid said.

"What you have to do is stop worrying about my state of mind and start to consider the trouble you're in if your boss, Estelle, finds out that you have the money."

"Estelle is no longer the boss," Omid said. "I am the boss."

"Congratulations," Freddie said. "Now we can go back and tell Charade Meade that the new boss stole their one million five hundred thousand dollars."

Omid looked astonished. "A million five? Is that what they're saying?"

"According to Charade."

"That's bullshit. There wasn't anything like that amount."

"That's the number Charade is looking to get back."

Omid's nervousness turned to anguish. "No, this isn't possible. She can't be saying that."

"How much would you say, Omid?"

Omid paused. His eyes darted around, as if looking for someone in the car who might be able to provide some support. He couldn't find anyone. "Maybe seven hundred and fifty thousand."

"Okay," Freddie said agreeably, "let's say it's seven hundred and fifty thousand. Give me the suitcase with seven hundred and fifty thousand. I believe I can sell that to Charade."

"I thought the two of you weren't legit," Omid said. "A couple of rip-off artists."

"Whatever we are, Charade wants the money back and she thinks we can get it for her. So far, she doesn't know about you. Let's make sure we keep it that way."

Silence in the car, broken only by the rain beating against the roof, Omid, mulling things over. "I can't get you the money tonight," he said finally.

"Omid, at this point I don't want to hear any more negatives, okay? I don't want you telling me what you can't do. I want you to tell me what you *can* do."

"I can get you the money," Omid said, "but it won't be until tomorrow."

"Listen to me again, Omid," Freddie said in the assertive voice Tree was slowly getting used to. "I can go back to Charade and say, I spoke to you and you said we'll have the money tomorrow. Do you want me to say that?"

"No, of course not."

"Then do better than 'tomorrow.'"

"Tonight. I can arrange for something tonight."

"This evening. At seven. The Lincoln Memorial. Come with the suitcase."

"Why there?" Omid demanded.

"It's public. That way you won't try anything and neither will we."

Omid nodded. "I think I can do that."

"You think, Omid," Freddie said. "Or you *can* do it?"

"I can do it," Omid mumbled.

"Good. That's what I wanted to hear. Now get out of the car, and we'll see you this evening."

Omid didn't say another word; he didn't even glance at Freddie or Tree. He simply opened the door and got out.

Freddie said to Tree, "What are you looking at?"

"I'm looking at you," Tree answered.

"What's that look on your face?"

"Amazement," Tree answered.

38

Late afternoon, and the rain had not stopped. Freddie and Tree had found a souvenir shop selling blue plastic ponchos. Now they wore them as they stood in front of a White House barely visible through the mist.

Despite the drizzle, tourists lined Pennsylvania Avenue snapping photographs. It was a world of picture-taking, the mob raising cellphones in the air to record everything. Where would it end? Thanks to technology, every moment of everyone's life was now digitally reproduced. The pictorial history of the era would be endless. Would anyone in the future care?

He glanced at Freddie beside him, holding the cheap umbrella they had purchased along with the ponchos, managing to look elegant and beautiful despite the miserable weather. No one, hopefully, would be recording them in the hours before they headed over to the Lincoln Memorial to retrieve a suitcase full of money.

"We are the only people who are not taking pictures of the White House," Freddie said, perhaps reading his mind.

"The Secret Service is probably running a check on us," Tree said. "What's wrong with those people? They aren't taking pictures."

"But they are on their way to pick up a suitcase stuffed with wads of hundred-dollar bills."

"Like you said, this is Washington," Tree reminded her. "All sorts of people could be getting paid off. Maybe that's why these people are out here. They are waiting for someone to pay them or they're about to pay someone. Everyone could be a crook and we just don't know it."

"There is a remote possibility they are just tourists."

"Crooked tourists," Tree pronounced.

They left the White House and took their time walking along 17th Street NW, past President's Park and the Eclipse, everything green and leafy and saturated with water. By the time they got to Constitution Avenue the rain had let up a bit.

They came onto the National Mall, through Constitution Gardens, the granite pillars and triumphal arches of the World War II Memorial, to the Lincoln Memorial Reflecting Pool. Through the mist, they could barely make out the distant Greek temple that was the Lincoln Memorial.

"We are going to be early," Freddie said.

"That's all right, gives us a chance to make sure the coast is clear."

Freddie squinted. "Right now it doesn't look so clear to me," she said.

"That's what I'm worried about," Tree said.

"Are you? Seriously?"

"This just seems awfully easy, that's all," Tree said. "Omid was a little too agreeable. Makes me nervous."

"Let's see what happens," Freddie said. "I've got my trusty gat with me. That's what gangsters call a gun, right, a gat?"

"You've watched too many old Warner Bros. movies," Tree said.

Rain-soaked but undeterred tourists choked the steps up to the memorial. Freddie and Tree squeezed through the throng. They reached the main chamber where the Great Man sat upon his Georgia white marble throne staring into the distance, a sight that always managed to impress Tree.

"He looks sad," Freddie observed standing at the barrier that kept the multitudes from getting too close to Abe.

"He probably doesn't like people receiving illicit cash under his nose," Tree said.

Freddie addressed the statue. "Sorry about this, Mr. President. We really are honest, Abe."

They turned away from the marble president and went through a pair of Doric columns. Omid was standing on the steps in his blue raincoat. He held a familiar suitcase in his right hand. He said, "Okay, I'm here."

"Give me the suitcase," Freddie said.

Omid hesitated. His rain-streaked face was a combination of anger and hesitation. Freddie said, "Omid? The suitcase."

Tree reached over and took the suitcase from Omid. "There you go," he said in a grudging voice.

He turned away, disappearing down the steps into the crowd.

Tree said, "Let's get out of here."

"What's the matter?" Freddie asked.

"I'm not sure," Tree said, "but something doesn't feel right."

They hurried down the steps. It was raining harder as they reached the mall. The Washington Memorial was an indistinct sketch in the distance. People surged and pushed around them, raising umbrellas, anxious either to get away from the Lincoln Memorial or up to it. Freddie grabbed Tree's arm.

They hurried past the Vietnam Veterans Memorial Wall and made their way onto Constitution Avenue, walking east, Tree leading the way. To where? he wondered. What were they running from? Or toward?

Something.

He was about to turn and ask Freddie to pick up the pace when a young man came abreast of him. He was pale and clean-shaven, wearing a windbreaker.

He said, "I want you to come to a stop and step to the curb."

"I'm sorry," Tree said, "what did you say?"

"Step to the curb," the young man in the windbreaker snapped. "Do it now."

An ambulance had stopped at the roadside. Three men dressed as paramedics jumped out. The man in the windbreaker grabbed at the suitcase. Tree yanked it away. The man in the windbreaker punched him in the stomach. Tree gasped and sank to his knees. The man in the windbreaker seized the suitcase. Strong hands lifted him up and propelled him forward. He had a moment to see the syringe and then there was a sharp prick of intense pain.

And then, nothing.

39

Tree's face was receiving a good licking.

He opened his eyes to find Clinton looming over him, his long ears dangling. When he saw that Tree had regained consciousness, he rose from his haunches. "There you are," Clinton said. "For a while there, I was worried about you."

"What happened?" Tree asked.

"They may have drugged you," Clinton answered.

"I wasn't sure if you could talk or not," Tree said. "I thought I might be imagining things. You know, a talking dog. How weird is that?"

"I only talk with you," Clinton said. "I keep quiet when that weird old guy is around, the one in the trench coat. He smells like stale cigarettes and whiskey. I don't like the way he smells. He should quit smoking. It's going to kill him one of these days."

"You're right about that," Tree said, sitting up. "Where am I?"

"You are where you usually are," Clinton said, "you're in trouble."

"I guess I am," Tree agreed.

"I wish you'd smarten up and learn to avoid getting into these situations. The cigarettes will kill that guy in the trench coat. Trouble is going to kill you."

"Don't worry about me," Tree said. "I'm going to be all right."

"But I do worry about you," Clinton said. "I worry because I don't think you're going to be all right. You don't realize it, Tree, but you're in the biggest mess you've ever been in—and that's saying something."

"What kind of trouble am I in?" Tree was trying to keep the sense of rising panic out of his voice, and, as usual, failing. "Do you know?"

He felt wet on his face. Not so much a tongue licking now as—what? Water falling? Yes, that was it. Water was dripping on his face.

Tree forced his eyes open. Darkness. A penumbra of light somewhere in the distance. Drops of water splashed against his forehead. He tried to move away. That seemed to take forever. He felt groggy, as though someone had drugged him, and quickly concluded that, in fact, someone had.

His stomach abruptly twisted and momentarily he thought he was going to be sick. He forced himself into a sitting position, and struck his head against a dripping overhead pipe. He groaned and fell back on a damp cement floor, holding his head.

After a while the pain subsided, although he still felt groggy, an artificial taste in his mouth, somehow otherworldly, as though floating in a void, a void that, from what he could see, fit into the narrow dimensions of a basement. Exposed stone walls disappeared into the darkness. A dank smell permeated his nostrils.

Tree used the rough stones to brace himself and then rise to his feet, an exercise that left him gasping. He listened for sounds coming from outside— nothing except the steady drip from the drain pipe. Where was he? Where was Freddie?

He remembered they were walking on Constitution Avenue. The ambulance, paramedics rushing him. Everything going dark—always darkest just before it goes completely black; words to live by. So now what?

He was hit by another wave of nausea. His knees buckled, and he sank to the floor again. A disembodied voice said, "Colonel Callan."

Tree raised his head.

The disembodied voice said: "Colonel Callan, glad you've regained consciousness. What happens in the next few hours will depend on your ability to cooperate with us. Do you understand that?"

"Who is Colonel Callan?" Tree's voice sounded small and hoarse in this dank basement.

"That is not the kind of question that makes us believe you are willing to cooperate," the voice said.

"If you're talking to me, I'm not Colonel Callan," Tree said.

There was a moment's silence before the voice resumed: "Colonel, there is a table in the corner. Please go to that table and open the drawer. Inside, you will find a hood. You will place that hood over your head, and await further instructions."

"Who are you?" Tree demanded. "What's going on? Where is my wife?"

"You know as well as we do that you are no longer married, Colonel. There is no wife. Now go to the table as directed and place the hood over your head."

"You're making a big mistake, Tree said.

The voice apparently didn't think so. "Colonel, I am not going to ask you again. Do as you are directed or there will be consequences."

Tree didn't have the strength for a second attempt at standing. Instead, he crawled over to the table in the corner. There was, in fact, a single drawer. He reached up and yanked it open. Inside was a piece of neatly folded black material. Tree pulled it out.

"That's it," the voice said. "Now place it over your head, and stay right where you are."

Tree did as he was told. The world descended once more into darkness.

Presently, he heard a sound. A door opening, heavy

bootsteps coming toward him. A voice—female this time—said, "Colonel, we're going to help you to your feet and then we're going to bind your hands. Is that understood?"

Tree didn't say anything. The female voice sounded impatient: "Is that understood, sir?"

"Yes," Tree said.

Hands lifted him roughly to his feet. His arms were pulled behind him, his wrists bound with what felt like plastic bands. The hands guided him forward. The people who were doing this said nothing. The sound of a door opening and then he was led up a flight of stairs. He stumbled at one point; the hands caught him.

Another door creaked open and he was guided along, footsteps echoing hollowly. Still another door opened. The scrape of a chair, and then hands pushed him down into a seated position followed shortly by the sound of a door closing. Then silence.

He sat in darkness.

40

The air reeked of stale cigarette smoke. Tree was having trouble breathing beneath the hood, and every time he sucked in air, his mouth filled with the awful taste of cigarettes.

After a while Tree did what he usually did in these situations—not that he had been in precisely this kind of situation before, but close enough.

He began to doze off.

His head fell forward and as soon as that happened, he jerked awake. Then it began again, the drowsiness, helped along by whatever they had pumped into him.

Someone coughing brought him back to consciousness.

More coughing before a door opened, somehow a welcoming sound. Footsteps crossed the room. A throat cleared ahead of another cough.

The hood was removed from Tree's head.

A table came into view. A metal ashtray was on it. A bearded man in his early thirties nodded at him and said, "Colonel, let's get your hands free so that you're a little more comfortable."

Colonel?

The bearded man ducked behind him and the next thing he knew his wrists were unbound. "There. That better?"

"Thanks." Tree shook his hands to get the blood flowing.

"No problem," said the bearded man as he seated himself across from Tree. The unkempt beard matched a full head of curly hair. He wore glasses, a blue T-shirt, worn jeans, and sneakers. The combination of the glasses and clothing made him look harmless enough, a college nerd hanging around on a Saturday afternoon, playing computer games, maybe watching a little football and having a few beers.

Except that's not what this guy was doing.

Seated, he put his hand to his mouth, and coughed into it. He smiled at Tree as he removed a pack of cigarettes and a Bic lighter from his jeans pocket and put them on the table beside the ashtray. He said, "Don't worry I'm not here to waterboard you or anything like that, Colonel, but I am going to smoke."

"I'm sorry you're going to smoke," Tree said.

"Tough bananas, as we say in the interrogation business." The bearded man grabbed the pack and shook loose a cigarette. He popped it in his mouth, picked up the lighter and set the cigarette alight. He sat back blowing smoke into the air. "My name is Dwayne, incidentally."

"I want to know that my wife is all right," Tree said.

"Colonel, apparently they've been through this with you. You are not married. There is no wife; no wife that we know of, and believe me, we know a lot.'

"Who are you?" Tree asked.

The Dwayne guy smiled and flicked ashes into the ashtray. "Someone who knows a lot," he said.

"You don't know everything," Tree said.

"Yeah? What don't we know?"

"For one thing, I'm not this Colonel what's-his-name."

"Callan. Colonel Frederick Callan."

"My name is Tree Callister, I'm a private investigator from Sanibel Island in Florida."

"We understand it's the cover you've been using, Colonel. But that's not who you are." The bearded man flicked more ashes in the direction of the ashtray. "If you want to know the truth, I'm quite an admirer of yours—that is, until you went rogue and disappeared. Funny, though. I was expecting someone a little more—I don't know, the actor who does those Dodge commercials? What's his name?"

"You mean Sam Elliott?"

"Yeah, that's the guy. Rugged, masculine kind of dude. You're sort of unprepossessing, if you don't mind my saying so. Probably works for you. In your line of work, you don't want to stand out too much."

"You've made a bad mistake," Tree said. "Get hold of my wife, Fredryka Stayner. She can verify my identity."

Dwayne smiled again and flicked more ashes into the ashtray. "Nice try, Colonel."

"Nice try? Are you insane?"

"You could argue I'd have to be insane to do this kind of work," Dwayne said with a smile.

"I have a wife, I have a life on Sanibel Island, I'm Tree Callister, I'm not Frederick Callan. Whoever he is." Did Tree's voice sound desperate? Yes, he thought, it did.

"We pick up an individual; he's not carrying any identification. No cellphone. No wallet. Nothing. Then that person tells us he's not who we know he is. You can imagine how I might be a tad skeptical."

"My wife was carrying my wallet and cellphone in her shoulder bag," Tree said.

"The wife you don't have," Dwayne said. He mashed the remains of his cigarette into the ashtray, and then flicked another out of the pack.

Tree watched how Dwayne stuck it in his mouth and fired up the Bic. "I wish you wouldn't smoke," Tree said.

Dwayne blew cigarette smoke into air already clogged with it. "Let's get past questions of identity, Colonel, and see if you can't help me with a couple of things. Cooperate with us and we will go a lot easier on you."

"Who are you?" Tree demanded.

"Like I told you before, I'm one of those people who know. I'm the guy who can make life very difficult if you choose not to cooperate."

"I don't know how I can do that when I'm not who you think I am."

Dwayne didn't say anything. Instead, he carefully balanced his lit cigarette on the edge of the ashtray and then rose and went around Tree and opened the door behind him. As soon as he was gone, Tree reached forward and doused the cigarette.

When Dwayne returned, he was carrying a familiar olive-green suitcase, Aston Martin Racing embossed on the side.

He placed the suitcase on the table, noticing the remains of his extinguished cigarette. His eyebrows moved up and down. "I wish you hadn't done that," he said to Tree. "You have any idea how much cigarettes are these days?"

"No, Dwayne, I don't," Tree replied.

"A fortune, let me tell you."

"I hate smoking," Tree said. "I can't stand the smell."

"I'm sorry to hear that," Dwayne said. He pointed at the suitcase. "So here's the thing, Colonel. You were caught red-handed accepting a suitcase full of money from an international gambling concern with ties to some pretty unsavory people in return for—what? Well, that's the question isn't it? That's one of the answers we are looking for before we send you to a federal prison for the rest of your life."

"Originally, I was hired by someone I went to high school with, Dan Meade."

"Yes, the former football player. A couple of seasons with the Bears as I recall. Not a great running back."

"I heard he was pretty good," Tree said.

"He might have been great, but then he decided to become a crook instead of a football player."

"Dan got involved in online sports betting. I knew that, but he said he was out of it."

"You know and I know, Colonel, Meade is not out of anything."

"I don't know," Tree said. "When I spoke to him he told me he's suffering from dementia, having trouble with his memory. He had a list of names and addresses—people in Savannah, in a place called Micanopy, and here in Washington. He didn't know why he had that list or what it meant. He wanted me to find out and report back to him."

Dwayne had to interrupt the ritual of his lighting another cigarette so that he could cough some more. "Excuse me," he said. The ashtray was beginning to fill up. "Incidentally, we believe Meade is lying. We don't think he has dementia."

Dwayne got his cigarette lit. "The thing is, in following the trail of this list, I ended up in Washington at what turned out to be a private club for sports betting," Tree explained. "They mistook my wife and me for couriers and handed over this suitcase. When they realized their mistake, they found out where we lived on Sanibel Island, broke into our house, and stole the suitcase."

Dwayne added more smoke to the air before he said, "That doesn't explain how you ended up at the Lincoln Memorial *accepting* the suitcase from Omid Serpiente, now does it, Colonel? Omid, I'm sure I don't have to tell you, is the conduit between the Dogin Group of Riyadh in Saudi Arabia and Meade's online bookmaking business—the business the Saudis and their Russian partners use to launder money."

"I didn't know any of this," Tree said. "I thought Omid was just a club employee who stole the money."

"I come back to what I asked you before, Colonel. If Omid stole the suitcase, what was he doing giving it back to you?"

The last part of his question was lost in a series of hacking coughs. Dwayne leaned forward pressing his hand against his chest. The coughing continued. Dwayne seemed to be having trouble breathing.

"Are you all right?" Tree said in alarm.

Dwayne waved a hand in front of him. "I'm fine, I'm okay," he insisted.

The coughing grew worse. Tree said, "Do you want me to call someone?"

Dwayne shook his head before he suddenly shot to his feet, losing his glasses, hand pressed against his chest again, gasping and choking for breath. Blood spewed out of his mouth onto the table, splattering the ashtray and the cigarette pack. Tree lurched up from his chair not certain what to do.

Dwayne gave Tree one last desperate look before his eyes rolled back in his head and he collapsed to the floor.

41

Dwayne lay still. The coughing had stopped. He was breathing heavily, but to Tree's relief, he was breathing. Tree saw the cellphone protruding from his interrogator's pocket. He reached down and took it, turned, and crossed the room to the door. He opened it expecting to be stopped by guards on the other side. But the long hall in which he found himself was empty. He went back into the room and grabbed the Aston Martin Racing suitcase. Dwayne groaned on the floor.

Lugging the suitcase, Tree went back into the hall. Still no one in view. He went along to the door at the end, opened it, and found himself on a stoop outside. It was dark. There was no one around.

He went down the steps and saw that he had been in a house in the middle of a field. He could see a distant forest, but no other houses. A Dodge Ram truck was parked not far from the stoop. No, he couldn't be that lucky. He tried the passenger door. It swung open. He looked inside. No key in the ignition. Instead, it lay in a cup holder. Yes, he thought, yes he *could* be so lucky.

He got behind the wheel, stuck the key into the ignition. The Dodge Ram growled to life. He thought of Dwayne who smoked too much, hoped he would be all right. Dwayne said Tree should look more like Sam Elliott. Well, here he was, driving Sam Elliott's Dodge Ram away from—where? Good question.

Where was he, anyway?

Right now that didn't matter. What did matter was escape. A narrow dirt track twisted into a thicket of trees. He followed the track through the trees and onto a highway. A GPS screen was mounted on the dashboard. Tree worked at the controls until a map appeared. The screen reported he was somewhere in Virginia.

Beside him on the seat Dwayne's cellphone vibrated, glowing in the dark. Tree looked at it. It continued to vibrate. Tree picked it up as he drove and swiped it open. "Dwayne?" a female voice said.

Tree thought about it for an instant and then coughed into the phone. "I was beginning to worry when I didn't hear from you," the voice said. "Are you all right? You sound awful."

"Fine," Tree said amid another cough.

"Look, it turns out we may be holding the wrong guy at the safe house. I'm not sure how it happened, but the man you're questioning isn't Callan. What's he telling you?"

"Same thing." Tree coughed some more.

"For heaven's sake, Dwayne," the female voice said. "You've got to do something about that cough."

"I'm okay," Tree said.

The female voice went silent. Then: "You sound funny."

"The cough," Tree said, amid more coughing.

"Who is this?" demanded the voice.

Tree shut down the phone as the road dipped toward the outskirts of a town. He came along what looked like the main street, buildings on either side darkened. He turned onto a side street and brought the truck to a stop. He picked up the phone again and punched out a number—hoping against hope.

"Hello?" Freddie's voice.

"It's me," Tree said.

"Tree, thank goodness," said Freddie, sounding vastly relieved. "Where are you? Are you all right?"

"Somewhere in Virginia. I'm okay. More or less. Where are you?"

"I'm sitting in our hotel room in Washington, frantic. Wondering what to do. I was just about to go to the police."

"Don't do that," Tree said. "I'm not sure what time it is or even what day it is."

"It's almost 10 p.m.," Freddie said. "They took you away yesterday."

"They didn't take you, obviously."

"I couldn't believe it," Freddie said. "They were so focused on you, they didn't notice me. One moment you were there. The next moment you were inside that ambulance disappearing into the traffic."

"They got the wrong guy," Tree said. "They thought I was someone else."

"Who's they?"

"I'm not sure," Tree said. "Maybe the CIA. Maybe NSA."

"The National Security Agency?"

"I don't know for sure," Tree said.

"CIA. NSA. Those aren't just any initials; those are spy agencies, Tree."

"Yes, I know that."

"What have we gotten ourselves into?"

"Right now I need to get to you."

"What happened? Did they let you go?"

"Not exactly," Tree said.

"What does that mean?"

"It means I escaped," Tree said.

"You escaped? From the NSA?"

"It wasn't very hard as it turns out, but in order to get away I had to steal one of their trucks."

"You stole a truck? From the NSA?"

"At least I think it's their truck. The point is, they're going to be looking for it before long."

"Tree, you should go to the police," Freddie said.

"I've got a suitcase full of money that doesn't belong to me, driving a stolen vehicle owned by people who are probably in charge of America's security. I don't think the police are an option right now."

"So what do we do?"

"I've got to get rid of this phone. They can probably track it. I won't call you again. I'm going to try to get to Washington. Once I'm there, I'll find a phone and call you. You can come and get me."

"Then what?"

"Then we'll figure out what to do next," Tree said.

42

The Dodge's GPS guided Tree onto I-66 toward Washington, Tree expecting flashing lights in his rearview mirror at any time. But the law enforcement agencies of Virginia apparently were unaware he was on the run, a wanted fugitive escaping across a darkened America in a stolen truck.

It struck him as he drove that lately he had been so busy trying to stay alive, he hadn't had a chance to think about dying. Instead, he felt curiously exhilarated. He was still alive. Against all odds. Maybe, just maybe, he could get out of this and back to the comparatively peaceful business of worrying about dying.

The traffic on the highway at this time of night was light. WTOP, the local news station, carried no breaking news of a citywide search for an escaped national security threat named Tree Callister.

He crossed the Theodore Roosevelt Memorial Bridge, and then came south on Virginia Avenue NW to Constitution. He found a parking lot off Constitution, pulled in and left the keys under the front seat. He opened the suitcase. The money was still there. He took out a hundred dollar bill, stuck it in his pocket and closed the suitcase again.

Carrying the suitcase, Tree walked along Constitution to 15th Street NW until he reached the Washington, the landmark hotel that had been around since 1918 and where he had stayed a couple of times back in the days when he was a reporter.

It was nearing midnight, and the lobby bar was packed with young, well-dressed Washingtonians not anxious to give up and go home to bed. He walked to where he remembered a bank of pay phones. Sure enough, the phones were still there. He went to the front desk, got change for his hundred-dollar bill and then returned to the phones. Freddie picked up immediately.

"Where are you?" Tree asked.

"Just getting the car," Freddie said. "Where are you?"

"At the Washington Hotel on Fifteenth. Can you come here?"

"I'm on my way," Freddie said.

Thirty minutes later, Freddie entered the lobby, waving when she saw him seated on one of the lounges. Her face drawn with a combination of concern and relief, she hurried over and embraced him, holding him tight. "I didn't know what to think," she said in a strained voice, "not knowing if you were alive or dead."

"I'm still alive, more or less," he said.

They sat together on the divan. Tree had already consumed a chicken salad sandwich and a Diet Coke. Freddie ordered a glass of sparkling water. Hotel life swirled happily around them while they luxuriated in the knowledge that they were reunited and—for a few minutes at least—safe.

"Tell me something," Tree said finally. "When you think of a rogue warrior, someone who's admired inside the intelligence community, a rugged tough guy, who would you think of?"

"I'm not sure what you're getting at," Freddie said.

"Someone you would think of."

"Rugged, you say?"

"Yeah, mature but rugged."

"I'd think of someone like that fellow who does the Dodge truck commercials. What's his name?"

"You mean Sam Elliott?"

"Yes, Sam Elliott. He's mature and kind of rugged, don't you think?"

"You wouldn't think of me?" Tree tried to keep the disappointment out of his voice.

Freddie looked at him for a beat or two before she said, "What's this all about?"

"Nothing." Tree tried to sound casual. "Something my interrogator, Dwayne, said to me, that's all."

"What did he say?"

"No big deal," Tree said. "He thought I looked unprepossessing."

"That's the word he used? Unprepossessing?"

"He was expecting someone named Colonel Callan to be more like Sam Elliott."

"But you're not Colonel Callan," Freddie said.

"No, I'm not."

"Then it shouldn't come as a surprise you didn't strike this guy as the Colonel Callan type."

"Yes, I suppose you're right," Tree said.

"On the other hand, it could be part of their brainwashing technique."

"Brainwashing?"

"Try to make you feel inadequate, break you down so that you would talk."

"You think that was it?"

"Had to be," Freddie said. "Of course, it didn't work."

"You don't think I look unprepossessing?"

Freddie smiled and said, "What? You think I would marry somebody who was unprepossessing?"

"Impossible," Tree said.

"Exactly," Freddie said. She rummaged around in her bag and then handed him his wallet and cellphone. "I've been keeping it charged just in case you called," she said. "It's rung a few times but every time I answer, the caller hangs up."

When the server brought Freddie her drink, Tree did

the best he could to answer the questions Freddie peppered him with. Not, as he repeated several times, that he knew a whole lot.

"As much as I could get from Dwayne the smoker, Dan Meade's offshore gambling enterprise is being financed by a Saudi syndicate called the Dogin Group of Riyadh. Dwayne said they are using online sports betting to launder money. That's brought it to the attention of the feds. Maybe that's why planes are blowing up and people are getting killed. It could be that Dan realized what was happening, made up some sort of list of people he had to warn before his illness overwhelmed him. But it was too late. He could no longer remember why he created his list."

"Which is where you came in," Freddie said. "Little did you know what sort of quagmire you were getting into."

"That's right," Tree said.

"But that doesn't explain why Omid would hand over the suitcase to us after going to all the trouble to steal it in Florida," Freddie said.

"Maybe he was working on his own, saw an opportunity to put a lot of money in his pocket. Then when we confronted him and said we were working for the Meade ladies, he had second thoughts and decided to give the money back—and that's when the feds swooped in."

"Thinking you're this Colonel Callan?"

"By now, they probably know that they made a mistake, but nonetheless they've got a fugitive who has escaped federal custody on their hands, so they are probably looking for me."

"There is a long list of people looking for you," Freddie said. "Yet here we are sitting in the lobby of a luxurious Washington hotel, sipping drinks, as though we don't have a care in the world."

"We could be in a Hitchcock movie, something by

Johnny Mercer playing in the background. Except I'm looking a little too scruffy. You, however, would be perfectly cast."

"Unfortunately, my darling husband, we are not in a Hitchcock movie. We are in yet another Tree Callister nightmare. The question is, how do we get out of it so that we don't end up spending the rest of our lives in a federal prison—a distinctly non-Hitchcock ending."

"We do what we're supposed to do," Tree said.

"And what exactly is that?"

"I've been hired to find this money." Tree put his hand on the suitcase beside him. "Okay, we've found it. Now let's deliver it to the clients—just like we agreed."

"I hate to say something as mundane as, 'I think we should go to the police.' But I think we should go to the police."

"We deliver the money, solve the mystery, bring the bad people to justice, and live happily ever after."

"I'm not so sure how happily we can live if we're dead," Freddie said.

Good point, Tree thought. He kept the thought to himself.

43

L ook kid," the guy in the snap-brimmed fedora hat said. "I don't want to rain on your parade or anything. But the fact of the matter is you do look kind of unprepossessing."

"You really think so?" Tree said.

"Look at my face. Rugged. Lived in. A face that's been around the block a few times, know what I mean? Your face? Your face never got around the block. What do you do? You sell insurance? You work in a bank? What?"

"I'm a private detective," Tree said.

The man in the fedora threw back his head and laughed. "Come on, kid. Don't kid a kidder. I'm a private detective. You're a bank teller."

"I'm not a bank teller," Tree protested.

"Well, you're no private detective. Hell, you're not even wearing a trench coat."

Freddie said, "Trench coat? What are you talking about?

Tree blinked awake. Freddie, fully dressed, was standing over him. "You were mumbling about trench coats," she said.

Tree struggled into a sitting position. A thin stream of sunlight seeped through a crack in the closed drapes to remind the weary guest it was now afternoon. They had stopped at a Hampton Inn outside Charleston off I-95 after driving most of the night. The exhausted fugitives had immediately fallen into a deep sleep.

Tree's cellphone began to vibrate on the nightstand next to the bed. He looked at it and groaned.

"You'd better answer it," Freddie said.

When he swiped it open a voice said, "Where the devil are you?"

"Who's this?" Tree said.

"It's your employer. Who do you think it is?"

"Charade?"

"Who else? Where have you been? And who is that woman who kept answering your phone?"

"That's my assistant," Tree said, fighting to clear his head.

Freddie frowned and mouthed, *I'm not your assistant.*

"As for where I've been, I've been in Washington doing what you hired me for."

"Have you found my money?"

"I'm on my way back now," Tree said.

"With the money."

"With the money."

"You're kidding," Charade said. "You've got the money?"

"You sound surprised," Tree said.

"I was worried when I couldn't get hold of you." He could hear her take a deep breath. "There's been a change in plan."

"What kind of change?"

"Don't bring the money back to Sanibel."

"Where should I bring it?"

"Micanopy. Easier for everybody. Doris and I will meet you there."

"Okay," Tree said. "But why there?"

"Call this number as soon as you get to town."

Charade hung up.

Freddie looked at him. "Well?"

"We're not going to Sanibel. They're waiting for us in Micanopy."

"Why do you suppose they want you there?"

"When I asked that question, Charade hung up on me."

"Showdown in Micanopy," Freddie said.

44

Shafts of golden light worked through the hanging moss on the live oaks forming a canopy over the roadway, so startlingly beautiful impressionable motorists might imagine they were on the road to paradise.

But then paradise was lost. Past a small white chapel, the world descended into a malignant green unreached by sunlight. Witches and ogres surely dwelled here, not to mention that seductive sorceress Charade Meade awaiting the arrival of her next victim. Was Tree to be that victim? The possibility loomed larger the closer he got to Micanopy.

Tree handed Freddie his cellphone. "Do me a favor. Bring up the last call."

"That would have been Charade Meade," Freddie said.

"That's right."

Freddie gave him a confused look but did as he asked. When it began to ring, she handed the phone to Tree.

"Where are you?" Charade demanded as soon as she came on the line.

"I want you to meet me at the Marjorie Rawlings homestead," Tree said.

"Why would you want to meet there?"

"Didn't you read *The Yearling* as a kid?"

"I read *Valley of the Dolls*," Charade said. "Why are you giving me such a hard time?"

"What about the Gregory Peck movie?" Tree asked. "Did you see that?"

"I didn't even know there was a movie," Charade answered irritably.

"The Marjorie Rawlings homestead," Tree repeated. "I expect you there in an hour."

Tree swiped the phone closed. He said to Freddie, "Here's what I would like you to do."

"The directions to Marjorie Rawlings's place?"

"I've always wanted to see where she wrote *The Yearling*. It was one of my favorite books as a kid."

"I never read it," Freddie said.

"Neither did Charade," Tree said. "Did you know there was a movie?"

"Of course," Freddie said. "With Claude Jarman Jr. and Jane Wyman."

"Very good," said Tree admiringly.

Freddie had her iPad open, hitting the Maps icon. "We're about an hour away," Freddie said.

"That should be just about right," Tree said.

I'm not sure what you're doing," Freddie said, her voice tight.

"Think about it," Tree said. "If we meet them in Micanopy who knows what we might be walking into. If we make them come to us out here, maybe we can control the situation and reduce our chances of getting into trouble."

"Any way you cut it, we're in trouble," Freddie said.

Three-quarters of an hour later, the toneless electronic voice emanating from Freddie's iPad, commanded a right turn onto County Road 325.

"Should be just ahead," Freddie announced.

"Are you all right?" Tree asked.

"I should have known that you, being you, wouldn't do what you were supposed to do."

"What was I supposed to do?"

"You were supposed to drive into Micanopy," Freddie said.

"Why? Because that's what Charade wants us to do?"

"It's all right," Freddie answered. "Forget I said anything."

"Something's wrong," Tree said.

"What could be wrong?" Freddie's voice had grown tense. "Up ahead, you are going to make a right turn."

Tree started to make the turn and as he did, the MRAP, a sand-colored behemoth coming at them from the opposite direction, smashed into the driver's side of the car. There was a loud whump accompanied by the sound of metal crushing. The hood buckled. Tree's air bag exploded and so did Freddie's.

Tree was aware of the car sailing off the road, across the shoulder, and down into a shallow gulley. Tree thought for sure the vehicle would go over onto its side. But then it managed to right itself, and settled, making groaning sounds, as though in great distress.

He heard the sound of a door opening, and that's when he saw Freddie slide out. Something moved to his left and a man wearing suspenders staggered into sight coming out of the MRAP. Will Mickens, out of his sheriff's uniform today, armed with a sawed-off shotgun, came around the hood of the MRAP.

Freddie, out of the car, gun in her hand, was firing at Will, who immediately let loose with the shotgun. The windshield was abruptly starred with buckshot. Freddie ducked down and fired a second shot that sent Will skittering back behind the MRAP.

By this time, Tree had managed to squeeze around the exploded airbags and crawl out the open passenger door. He crouched beside Freddie, pain shooting through his left leg.

"Are you all right?" Freddie asked.

"What the hell does Will think he's doing?" Tree said.

"I don't know, but I'm not going to take the time to ask him." Freddie fired another shot in the direction of the MRAP. "You get into those trees while I cover you."

"Why am I doing that?"

"So we can get to the Rawlings place where there will be people and Will won't try to kill us anymore."

She fired another shot that caused a loud twanging sound as it ricocheted off the side of the MRAP. "Go," Freddie ordered

Tree jumped up, the pain shooting along his leg, and hobbled toward a stand of trees, certain that at any moment, he would be shot. But he reached the cover of the trees safely and turned to find Freddie right behind him. "Keep going," she whispered.

Gun in hand, she helped him limp through the trees until they reached an unpaved roadway Marjorie Rawlings must have once walked on. They pushed through a rusty gate, past spectacular groves of fruit trees, an open barn with a view of a buckboard, and roosters strutting and pecking at the lawn fronting a pair of one-story wood-frame cottages. But no people.

"Where is everyone?" Tree asked.

Freddie lowered Tree next to one of the oaks, where they had an unobstructed view of the roadway. Tree groaned in pain and said, "There's no one here. Nothing to stop him from coming after us."

"You know that, and I know it," Freddie countered. "But Will doesn't. Besides, he's going to see the suitcase in the car. That's what he's after."

"My brilliant plan didn't work very well," Tree said.

"Apparently not," Freddie said. She gave him one of her skeptical looks. "Exactly what was your brilliant plan?"

"To force Charade out here so we wouldn't be in danger in Micanopy."

"She sent Will with a shotgun instead."

They waited behind the tree, keeping an eye on the road and the surrounding grounds. Waiting.

But no one came.

After an hour, Tree's leg was feeling better. He stood on it, discovered he wasn't limping so much.

"Maybe we should check the road," he said.

"All right," Freddie agreed. "We're not accomplishing much sitting here."

Together, they cautiously made their way back to the highway, keeping to the trees in case Will appeared with his shotgun. They reached the crumpled twisted wreck of their car—a reminder that when you encountered a monster military vehicle, the outcome was not good. There was no sign of Will Mickens or the MRAP. The Aston Martin Racing suitcase was not in the backseat. Freddie retrieved the carryall from the trunk.

"Let's see if we can find a ride into Micanopy," Freddie said.

Tree said, "You seem anxious to get into Micanopy."

Freddie kept her eyes on the road. "Where else would you like to go, Tree?"

Before he could answer, a battered pickup truck came into view and pulled to a stop. A small man, gnome-like, completely bald, with the crafty face of a gambler able to read the cards of life and play them to his advantage, rolled down his window. "Looks like you folks are having some trouble."

"A fellow smacked into us and then drove away," Tree said.

"Did quite a job on your car," the gnome-like man said. "Looks like a write-off."

"We could sure use a ride into Micanopy."

"I think I can help you out," said the gnome-like man. "Hop in."

45

The gnome-like man said his name was Walter Bird. "I grew up around these parts," Walter explained as he drove. "Out by Cross Creek. Still got some land out there, in fact."

"Do you live here?" inquired Freddie, seated beside him.

"Not for years," answered Walter. "But I like to come back every so often. Refreshes me, reminds me of my roots."

"Where do you live now?" Freddie asked.

"Here and there," Walter said. "I'm the type of fella likes to keep moving. What about you folks? Tourists are you?"

"From Sanibel Island," Freddie said.

"Nice place," Walter said. "Shame that you folks drive all the way up here, only to have one of the locals smash up your car like that."

"It's a rental," Freddie said. "So I guess it's not the end of the world."

"Least you folks weren't hurt, and that's to the good."

"Yes it is," Freddie agreed.

"It's getting dark. Where can I drop you?"

"If you could take us to Cholokka Boulevard, that would be great," Freddie said.

Walter gave her a quizzical glance. "I can do that. Sure you don't want me to take you to a hotel?"

"No, that's fine," Freddie said. "We have friends who can meet us there."

"Locals? Anyone I'd know?"

"People we're traveling with," Freddie said too hurriedly.

Walter gave her another look. "Too bad they couldn't have picked you up out at the Rawlings place."

"We were just going to phone them when you happened along," Tree interjected.

"You've been a lifesaver," Freddie said.

Walter brought his truck to a stop when he reached Cholokka Boulevard. "There you go," he said. "Sure you're gonna be all right?"

"We'll be fine," Freddie said. "Thanks for all your help."

"Much appreciated," added Tree.

"Take care of yourselves," Walter said. "Go careful in this dark world."

He drove off, leaving Freddie and Tree at the side of the road. "I can't believe you wanted to come back here," Tree said.

"Trust me," Freddie said.

"Because you know what you're doing?"

"I wouldn't go that far," Freddie said.

In the light from a half moon, the Mickens house appeared more exhausted and lost than ever.

A single light glimmered on the ground floor.

They stood together at the corner, surveying the house, Tree holding the carryall, a couple of visitors to Micanopy, confused, wondering where to go. Except Freddie seemed to know. "Let's see who's inside," she said.

"Why would you want to do that?"

"Open up the carryall," Freddie said.

Tree looked at her and then unzipped the bag. It was full of money.

Tree shook his head and said, "When did you do this?"

"Back at the hotel. While you were sleeping," she said.

"I'm afraid Will's got most of our clothes, not to mention one of the hotel's ice buckets."

"You're not telling me everything," Tree said.

"Don't argue with me about this," Freddie said brusquely, and started off toward the house. Tree hesitated a moment, not sure what to do.

Then he followed his wife.

A mass of trees, shadows against the night sky, framed the yard at the rear of the house. There was a small porch and a back door that opened when Tree pressed the latch. He stepped inside, Freddie crowding behind him. She held the Glock. He was getting used to her with that gun, something he previously never would have expected.

Music came to them from deep in the house. Freddie said in a whisper, "That sounds familiar. Where have I heard it before?"

"It's the theme from *Charade*," Tree said.

A chorus began to sing:

Sad little serenade
Song of my heart's composing
I hear it still, I always will
Best on the bill
Charade…

As the music continued, they went through a large kitchen, along a creaking corridor toward the light. They entered the parlor, empty except for an open coffin mounted on a pair of sawhorses.

The light from a standing lamp threw long shadows across the walls as Freddie and Tree approached the coffin.

Inside, hands neatly folded across her stomach, lay Doris Meade.

Beside the coffin was an olive-green suitcase.

"It was her favorite music," Charade said, coming in from the far side of the room. She wore a short black dress. Her blond hair floated around her shoulders. "She said each time she heard it, the song made her think of me."

"Dan Meade likes that song, too," Tree said.

"Personally, when it comes to Johnny Mercer, I like 'Moon River' a lot better," Charade said.

"Did you kill her?" Tree asked.

Charade advanced into the room, making a face. "I loved Doris," Charade said. She gave Freddie an admiring look. "A beautiful woman with a gun. You've married up, Tree."

"That's for sure," Tree said.

"You didn't answer my husband's question," Freddie said.

Charade shook her head, "Doris had a stroke yesterday, shortly after we arrived back in Micanopy. If I were going to kill her it certainly wouldn't be over money in a suitcase. In the scheme of things, that's nothing. However, I'm dealing with people who don't like to be ripped off."

"The Dogin Group?" Tree said.

"Deep pockets, but ruthless," Charade said. "Sonny Picas needed financing and brought them in. Dan didn't like that. He felt they were trying to push him out. And they certainly were. They blew up his jet when they thought he was going to be onboard."

"What was the list for?" Freddie asked.

"Dan put together a list of people he could count on to side with him against Sonny and his investors," Charade said. "Unfortunately, after Dan became ill, he couldn't remember why he had prepared it, and, unknown to Doris and myself, made the silly mistake of hiring your husband. Then we compounded the error by hiring him ourselves."

"And here we are tonight," Freddie said.

Charade nodded toward the carryall in Tree's hand.

"Finally returning the money, just as you were hired to do," she said.

That was the cue for Will Mickens to step into view, leveling his shotgun at Freddie and Tree. Will said, "Be careful of that damned woman over there. She's got a gun and she's a little too anxious to use it."

"I'm surprised how easy it is to shoot at the people pointing guns at my husband and me," Freddie said.

"Better if you put your gun on the floor," Charade said.

"I don't think so," Freddie said in a preternaturally calm voice. "That's all the incentive Will needs to shoot the two of us."

"Let's all stay calm," Charade said. "No need for guns."

"Glad to hear it," Tree said.

"The money in your carryall," Charade offered, "why don't you take it with you when you leave?"

"Money for a job well done?" Tree said.

"Call it the cost of compromise," Charade said. "Like I said, in the scheme of things, it's nothing. This way everyone leaves with a smile."

"Will's not smiling," Freddie said, "and he's not lowering that shotgun."

"That's for damn sure," Will said.

There was a commotion outside followed by an explosion of splintering wood and breaking glass. Will jerked around. Tree lunged at him, knocked the shotgun away as Will pulled the trigger. It went off with a bang that shook the room. Tree heard Charade scream before the force of the shotgun blast sent her flying back against the coffin.

Tree punched furiously at Will. He tumbled to the floor. A swarm of figures descended. Tree caught a fleeting glimpse of Dwayne before he was engulfed and thrown to the floor, his arms yanked behind him. Someone yelled, "Don't move, Callister. Don't move."

Tree did as he was ordered. Freddie was frozen in place, staring down at Charade crumpled across the coffin, bleeding onto the body of Doris Meade.

46

As soon as they were in the yard behind the house, Dwayne removed the handcuffs other officers had put on Tree. Freddie, not nearly the menace to society represented by her husband, had been allowed to go without handcuffs.

Once the cuffs were off, they sat on a wrought-iron bench in moonlight beneath an impressive live oak—the perfect setting for serenading your sweetheart, Tree mused. Except he didn't have his ukulele with him; there would be no serenading this evening.

Freddie and Tree sat together in numbed silence watching various law enforcement officials entering and exiting the house. Blinking lights from a fleet of police vehicles lit the front. Dwayne, in his usual T-shirt and jeans, came out of the house, followed by a second man. Tree started when he saw that it was the gnome-like Walter Bird. Tonight, Walter looked much more professional in a rumpled sports jacket and tie.

"Don't tell me," Tree said to him. "You're not from around here."

Walter smiled and said, "I grew up in Alachua County, out at Cross Creek. And what I said is true, I still own land around there, been in my family for generations. I guess the only thing I wasn't quite honest about was my name."

"You're not Walter Bird?"

"I am Walter," he said. "Except I haven't been myself for a while."

"Walter heads the Savannah office of the FBI,"

Dwayne explained. "But for the past year or so he's been doing undercover work inside the Dogin Group."

"Where I was known as A.T. Kamala."

"You're A.T. Kamala?" Freddie said in surprise. "You were in Washington?"

"Like I told you before, I'm here and there."

"Walter allowed himself to be recruited by Will Mickens about a year ago. He's been working with us on this investigation ever since," said Dwayne.

"An investigation that has come to a more or less satisfactory conclusion," Walter said. "Will Mickens has been arrested for murder, among other charges. We couldn't have done it without your help."

"A woman is dead in there," Freddie said in a shaky voice. "I don't see how that's a satisfactory conclusion."

"I'm sorry about that," Walter said. "Things got somewhat unpredictable. It happens in a situation like this."

"A situation like this wasn't supposed to happen," Freddie said. She took Tree's hand in hers, held it tight.

Walter sat beside them on the bench while Dwayne stayed on his feet. "There is one piece of this that's missing," Walter said.

"What's that?" Tree said.

"We still don't know the whereabouts of Dan Meade," Walter said.

"Can you help us with that, Tree?" Dwayne said.

"I don't know where he is," Tree said.

Walter didn't hide his disappointment. "Are you sure? He's been in touch with you, hasn't he?"

"Yes, but he never says where he is," Tree pronounced.

"If he calls you again, try and find out his location," Walter said. "Could you do that for us?"

"After tonight, I can't imagine I'm going to hear from him," Tree said.

"But if he does."

"I'm not sure about anything," Tree said. "I'm not even sure what's happened." He looked at Freddie. "The part you played in all this."

"Freddie has been a great help to us," Dwayne said. "None of this could have succeeded without her."

Freddie leaned against Tree. A tear rolled down her cheek. "I want to go home," she said. "This isn't fun anymore."

Tree looked at Dwayne. "You mistook me for a guy named Frederick Callan."

"The NSA specializes in making stupid mistakes on occasion," Dwayne acknowledged. "That was one of them."

"Who is he?"

"If I told you that," Dwayne said, "we'd have to kill you."

At least he said it with a smile.

47

The big plastic container was under the desk, exactly where Tree had left it.

His kidneys.

He'd forgotten all about them. His kidneys seemed a long time ago. The least of his concerns. He lifted the can onto his desk. He was sitting there contemplating it when he received the news alert from the *Savannah Morning News* on his laptop he had been waiting for: the house on Bull Street had been sold.

"So let me get this straight," Rex Baxter said, once he settled into the visitor's chair. It was Rex's first day back at work since suffering his heart attack—or myocardial infarction, as Rex's doctors preferred to call it. He looked pale and it was obvious he had lost weight.

Rex continued, "Freddie conspired with the feds to gather evidence against Dan Meade's ex-wives."

"I think they were hoping to snare one of the Russians or Saudis involved in the Dogin Group," Tree explained. "The NSA believes they were using online sports betting to launder money and finance terrorist activities."

"You're kidding. The NSA is involved?"

"It's a matter of time before they ask me to join and become a secret agent."

"Aren't you a little old for James Bond?"

"I see myself more like Patrick McGoohan in that 1960s British TV series, *Danger Man*. They called it *Secret Agent* here in America. McGoohan was the last word in cool. You believed he could handle just about anything."

"Yeah, well, I'm sorry to tell you this, but I look at you and I believe you can't handle much of anything. I mean, Freddie orchestrated all this, right?"

"When they snatched me off the street in Washington, she realized what had happened, and convinced them to release me from that safe house after agreeing to cooperate."

"So you didn't really escape," Rex said.

"It felt like an escape to me," Tree said.

Rex rolled his eyes. "The other thing I can't believe, although I suppose I can, is that you got Freddie involved in this—and that when all the chips were down, she saved your sorry ass."

"I wouldn't go so far as to say that," Tree said.

"What would you say?"

"I'd say we make a great team," Tree said. "That's what I would say."

"She being the team member with a gun," Rex said.

"To my amazement," Tree said.

"Mine, too. The last person in the world I would expect to be packing heat."

"It was a once-in-a-lifetime thing," Tree said.

"So Freddie's not joining the Sanibel Sunset Detective Agency?"

Tree shook his head. "I'm a lone wolf."

Rex rolled his eyes again. "Yeah, right. What about Dan Meade?"

"What about him?"

The feds haven't found him?"

"No, but it's a matter of time," Tree said.

"Well, you and Freddie have certainly caused quite a stir. Jet blowing up. People dead. Illegal gambling. Terrorists."

"All in a day's work," Tree said.

"I should never have gotten sick," Rex said. "At least when I am around, you confine the messes you get into more or less to Sanibel Island. I turn my back, and you're in trouble all over the country."

"How are you feeling?" Tree asked.

"I'm okay," Rex said, "except I'm having intimations of mortality. Until recently, I thought I would live forever. Now I'm not quite so sure." He pointed to the plastic container on Tree's desk. "What about you? I see you still haven't pissed in your pot."

"Funny, before Dan Meade called, I worried about death all the time. Now I don't worry about it. Nearly getting killed makes you glad to be alive."

"Except that nearly getting killed can, in fact, get you killed, no matter how you think about it."

"Good point," Tree said.

Rex rose unsteadily from the chair. "Anyway, it's good to have you back giving tourism on Sanibel a bad name."

Tree looked at him. "Are you sure you're all right?"

"I'm not sure of anything," Rex said with a wan smile. "I've got to take it easy for the next while, so make sure you don't do anything to upset me."

"I'll do my best," Tree said.

Rex considered his old friend. "Are *you* all right?"

"Don't I seem all right?" Tree said.

"You seem distracted," Rex said.

"Thinking about something, that's all," Tree said.

"A dangerous pastime where you're concerned," Rex said.

———

After Rex left, Tree sat quietly in his office. For the four hundred thousandth time he studied the picture on the wall of the beauty in a bikini catching swordfish. The young woman would go on catching that swordfish forever. She would never grow old; she would always be lovely, the ideal of the South Florida beach babe who, in addition to looking great, could catch a fish.

Tree Callister would not catch a fish, and he had already grown old. He would not go on forever. He would pee into plastic containers. A sadness overwhelmed him as he sat listening to his heart beat. That heart could stop at any moment. His doctor had been "concerned." Something was going to happen, that much was certain; it was only a matter of time before they came for him.

There was only one thing to do.

He picked up the plastic container and put it back under his desk. Then he opened his laptop, brought up the screen he had previously bookmarked. No doubt about it. The house had been sold.

Tree rose from his desk. For now, he would not say anything to anyone. He was probably out of his mind. Well, there was no *probably* about it, was there?

He went down the steps out the back to where he had parked his rental Ford Taurus. He got in the car and drove across the causeway and then headed for the airport.

There was an American Airlines flight at three o'clock. He bought a return ticket and then spent an hour thumbing through the books and magazines at Coastal News before boarding his flight.

Everything was on time. The flight was smooth. He rented a car at the airport and drove into town. Beside him on the seat, the sound he was dreading the most—his cellphone vibrating. It was, as he suspected, Freddie.

"Am I missing something here?" she said, working hard to keep her voice calm and reasonable.

"What would you be missing?"

"I seem to be missing your exact location," she said.

"Why would you be missing that?"

"Because Rex just called to say that you disappeared in a puff of smoke."

"No smoke was involved," Tree said.

"Tree," Freddie said in her sternest voice, "where are you?"

"I'm in Savannah," Tree said.

There was a long pause before Freddie said, "What are you doing?"

"There is something I've got to check out. It's probably nothing. A wild hunch. I thought it would be better, and there would be less argument, if I just hopped on a plane."

"I thought we were doing this together," Freddie said.

"We have done it all together," Tree said. "I wouldn't be doing this if it weren't for your help and support."

"I don't care," Freddie answered. "I don't want this—you're either not telling me the truth or going off half-cocked without saying anything."

"I'm sorry," Tree said. "This won't take long. I should be back tomorrow. I'll explain everything then."

"I don't like what you're doing," Freddie said. "I have a bad feeling about this."

"There's nothing to worry about, believe me. I love you."

There was silence.

48

The handsome red-brick house at 429 Bull Street stood across from Monterey Square: arched windows, a cast-iron fence, a sense of courteous old Savannah opulence.

Tree opened the gate. Trimmed hedges flanked the walkway. He mounted steps to a front door set between Grecian columns and matching coach lights. He rang the bell and waited.

The door opened and Dan Meade leaned out, his complexion pink and healthy, highlighting a welcoming smile. "Tree," he said. If he was surprised to see his old high school chum, he managed not to show it.

"Hello, Dan. Can I come in?"

Dan stepped back and opened the door wider to allow Tree entry. The tiled foyer, stripped of furniture, echoed with their footsteps. Tree followed Dan into a parlor, bare of furniture except for a forlorn-looking couch positioned in front of a marble fireplace. The floors were dusty. Faded squares over the fireplace and along the walls showed where paintings had been hung.

Tree said, "This is where Johnny Mercer grew up, right?"

Dan smiled and nodded. "How did you find me?"

"Not so hard as it turned out," Tree said. "I kept an eye on the local newspaper after I saw that the Mercer House was up for sale. This morning there was a report the place had been sold. I figured you were the one person in the world who would buy it, no questions asked."

Tree looked around. "I guess you haven't had much time to redecorate."

"It has been a busy time," Dan agreed.

"What with your Russian and Saudi backers in the Dogin Group deciding they didn't need you any longer."

"Is that your guess, Tree?"

"They were getting nasty—blowing up your jet was probably all the proof you needed. Not to mention the feds who were closing in and about to charge you with crimes that could send you to prison for the rest of your life."

"That was a possibility," Dan said agreeably.

"You thought you were fine. As far as you were concerned, you were no more suffering from dementia than I was. But you wanted everyone to think you were—your capacity diminished, no threat to your enemies. That made a number of things easier, including sticking a knife into Prudence Colt."

"Why would I do that?" The question was calmly asked.

"Perhaps you discovered she was working for the Dogin Group, or maybe you thought she knew the truth about you and was in the way."

"Or maybe I'm just plain nuts," Dan said.

"I don't think you're nuts, but you are sick and getting sicker. You really couldn't remember why you made that list, and that's why you hired me. It didn't mean much, as it turned out, but that's beside the point.

"You've done a pretty good job of hiding until now," Tree continued. "But if I can find you, so can the people who want you dead."

"Maybe you're one of those people," Dan said.

"I came here to help you, Dan, to make sure you're safe."

"You're lying," Dan said quietly. "You're no better than the rest of them. They want to get me, so they sent you here to lure me out of hiding."

"Dan, that's not true."

"Are they waiting outside? Is that it?"

"I came alone. No one knows I'm here."

Dan gave Tree a glassy smile and said, "It's a sad little serenade."

He glided to the fireplace. Tree noticed a carved wooden box atop the mantel. "I hear it still and I guess I always will."

"Dan, what are you doing?"

Dan opened the lid of the box. Tinkling music rose from its interior: the theme from *Charade*. "A wonderful Henry Mancini song," Dan said. "Brilliant lyrics, as usual, from Johnny Mercer. Not as well-known as some of Johnny's other work, but my all-time favorite."

He withdrew something from the box and when he turned, he was holding a small pistol in his hand.

"We did play out this charade, Tree. Playing at games, acting out names. And I must say you did a pretty good job guessing the parts everyone played."

"Dan," Tree said, trying to keep his voice level. "I'm not your enemy. I'm your friend, remember? We went to high school together. You told me I was the only person you could trust."

"That was then, Tree, before you betrayed me, betrayed our friendship."

"Dan, please. Put the gun down."

"Johnny Mercer is right. Fate really is pulling at the strings. They all believe my capacity is diminished. Head injuries from football. So sad. A tragedy. And then Tree Callister broke in, unexpected, and Dan, poor Dan, scared, not himself, and the gun was in his hand, and he didn't recognize his friend, and this was an intruder and he thought he was protecting himself, like any law-biding citizen has the right to protect himself. What's it called here? Stand your ground?"

"Dan—"

"Now it's time for me to be gone. But, just like the song says, the music box plays on…"

The gunshot was no more than a loud pop, echoing in the all-but-empty room. For a moment, Tree wasn't sure what had happened. He looked at Dan Meade for some sort of confirmation, but Dan just smiled that glassy, other-worldly smile and lowered the gun he was holding.

Then the pain hit, a white-hot poker digging deep into his chest. Tree staggered backward, having trouble breathing. Dan, a few feet away, went out of focus.

Everything swirled around, bright colors dancing in the air. The colors cleared and abruptly the room was far below. Tree could see Dan move toward the body on the floor. Then Dan was gone and the body, too. Tree found himself walking through a long tunnel.

A guy in a trench coat wearing a snap-brimmed fedora lit a cigarette and smiled sardonically. "Welcome to the club, kid," the man in the fedora said. "We've been waiting for you. You can stop worrying. It's time to sleep the big sleep."

Then a dog was loping along beside him, a hound with long, floppy ears. "Clinton," Tree called. "What are you doing here?"

"Making sure you're okay," Clinton said. "Come on, follow me."

And Clinton leapt ahead, bounding toward a brightening light. Tree called his name again and then started after him, the two of them together, a man and his beloved dog, racing toward the light.

49

Tree came awake with a jolt.

"What light are you talking about?" Rex Baxter said.

"I'm not sure," Tree said groggily. "I was in a dark tunnel, running toward a light. I was with a dog."

"A dog. What kind of dog?"

"A hound, I think. I'm not sure." He twisted his head toward Rex. "What are you doing here?"

Rex gave an ironic smile. "Good question. I guess I thought I'd better drop around and make sure you're all right. Not that I'm interested in your well-being or anything."

"I thought you were in this bed, not me," Tree said.

"No sir. You're the one who had a heart attack."

"Heart attack?" Tree said in alarm. "I didn't have a heart attack. Someone shot me—again."

"Shot you?" Rex issued a snort of laughter. "Well, that's one way of looking at it, I suppose."

"Tell me what happened."

"You don't remember?"

"Not much, no."

"You no sooner arrived at WBBM where I was preparing my vastly popular weather forecast—sunny skies over Chicago with just a hint of cloud cover, temperatures rising to seventy-five degrees in the afternoon—than you started having chest pains. The next thing, you collapsed in my office. An ambulance was called, by Kelly—your ex-wife, incidentally."

"Kelly called the ambulance?"

"While I held you and whispered sweet nothings."

"Probably saved my life, those sweet nothings."

"The ambulance and the hospital might have had something to do with it, too," Rex said. "The doctors say you're going to be okay. You just have to take it easy for a while."

Freddie appeared at the door, holding a vase full of spring flowers. She wore a matching ivory jacket and skirt. She looked like a white angel—a slightly nervous angel. "Hi," she said. "Am I interrupting something?"

"No, no," Rex said. "Come on in. I was just getting ready to leave."

Freddie stepped tentatively into the room. "I brought you some flowers." She held up the vase as if to provide proof.

"That's very kind of you," Tree said.

Freddie plunked the flowers down on the window sill as Rex rose to his feet. "Take care of yourself," he said to Tree. "I'll drop back tomorrow and make sure you're still alive."

"They can't kill me," Tree said. "There would be no one to make sure you behave."

"I think it's the other way around," Rex said with a grin. "But I'd better not give any secrets away just yet." He looked at Freddie. "It's nice to see you again."

"Good to see you, Rex," she said.

After Rex left, Freddie seated herself beside the bed and Tree said, "I hate you seeing me like this."

"I must admit you looked much better a couple of weeks ago at that dinner party," she said. Then she took his hand in hers. Her hand felt warm and welcoming. "But I'm just glad you're going to be all right."

"I've been having the strangest dreams," he said.

"It's probably the anesthetic."

"We were married—in my dream," Tree said.

"Wow," she said with a smile. "That was fast."

"We were married and living on an island in Florida. Sanibel Island."

"Never heard of it," Freddie said.

"My mother and aunt used to take my brother and me there when we were kids. It's off the west coast of Florida."

"So in your dream we are married and living on an island." She smiled again. He was awed by that smile. He could survive anything in the glow of her smile.

"Here's the weird part," Tree continued. "I was a private detective on Sanibel."

"You weren't in the newspaper business?"

Tree shook his head. "I can't imagine it. I mean, I've been writing for newspapers since I was a teenager. How I managed to end up a private detective on Sanibel Island, I'll never know."

"It was just a dream," Freddie said. She held his hand tighter.

"I was the Sanibel Sunset Detective," he said.

"Were you now?"

"Probably read too many pulp-fiction detective novels as a kid," Tree said. "But Rex was there, too."

"He was also a private eye?"

"No, I think he was the president of the chamber of commerce on the island."

"Boy, that was some dream," Freddie said.

"It seemed so real," Tree said. "There was also a big hound dog named Clinton."

"A dog named Clinton?" Freddie said.

"A talking dog," Tree said.

"That's some imagination you've got there, Mr. Callister."

"Call me Tree. All my friends do."

"Yes, well, all my friends are wondering how I can date a guy named Tree."

"What did you tell them?"

"I told them that going out with a guy named Tree isn't so bad."

He looked at her and said, "This is going to sound really mushy."

"And hard-nosed Chicago newspapermen should never sound mushy, right?" Freddie said. "But go ahead. Be mushy. I promise not to tell anyone."

"I was going to say something like, with you here I know I'm going to be fine."

Freddie's brow wrinkled. "That didn't sound so mushy."

"The better I feel, the mushier I get," Tree said.

"Then maybe I'll stick around for that," Freddie said. "I kind of like you mushy."

"What about when I'm not mushy?" Tree said.

"You have your moments," Freddie said.

"I like the part where you said you are going to stick around."

"As long as you don't end up a detective on an island I've never heard of," Freddie said.

"It was just a dream, quite vivid, but no more than that," Tree said.

"Just a dream," Freddie murmured, rising from her seat. "This is the part that's real."

She kissed him on the mouth. The kiss seemed to go on forever.

Yes, he thought, this is real.

Acknowledgments

Humphrey Bogart died in 1957 at the age of fifty-seven, killed by the cigarettes you invariably see him smoking. But in fact he never died. Thanks to the movies, he lives on forever. Film has achieved what thousands of years of medical science could not—immortality for a select few.

I did briefly meet Bogie's widow, Lauren Bacall, who co-starred with him in some of his most memorable and iconic films, including *To Have and Have Not* and *The Big Sleep*. Bacall tripped over my foot at a Detroit cast party for *Applause*, the musical that was to win her a Tony award on Broadway.

By then Bogart had been gone for nearly thirteen years, but he was certainly not forgotten. In those days before DVDs or streaming on demand, audiences rediscovered Bogie in repertory cinemas. The cynicism, the battered romanticism, the "tough without a gun" nonchalance he was able to strike seemed utterly contemporary to youthful audiences sitting in darkened theaters, bathed in glorious black and white. Bogie, briefly, was a hero for the times.

The reality was something entirely different. Reality was a short, balding actor who, rather than growing up on the mean streets of New York (as had Jimmy Cagney, for instance), was born on the Upper East Side to well-to-do parents (his father was a wealthy doctor; his mother a famous illustrator) and who got his start in theater usually playing the sort of young swell who bounded on stage asking, "Tennis, anyone?"

Reality was something of a sourpuss, a bad drunk who could get pretty ugly with a couple of drinks in him (before

Bacall, he and his previous wife were known as the Battling Bogarts), a complainer who managed never to be very happy with his life as a contract player at Warner Bros.

That is not the reality Tree Callister encounters in *Heart of the Sanibel Sunset Detective*. Tree gets the iconic Bogie, the stuff of the movie legend that drew me to him as a teenager.

I owe him a lot when it comes down to it. The old *Toronto Telegram*, my favorite newspaper in the world, one year ran a biography contest. The winner got a summer job in the *Telegram* newsroom. I wrote about the life of Humphrey Bogart and submitted it to the paper. I didn't win the job, but I was a runner-up, and that gave me the confidence to believe I might have a life in the newspaper business. If it wasn't for Bogie, who knows what might have happened to me.

The Bogart who fascinated a small-town teenager holds up remarkably well today, even though the years have diminished his cult-like status. The celluloid dreams that kept previous generations enthralled don't much interest a contemporary audience that ignores anything not in color—and Bogie lives in black and white.

Tree is part of a diminishing crowd holding onto the memories of another, some would say better, movie age. Those memories are fragile and fast slipping away. Will anyone even remember Bogart or any of his contemporaries after the Baby Boomers are gone? That's anyone's guess, but for the moment, Bogie remains a useful supporting player helping Tree as best he can to survive his latest adventure.

As has been the case previously when these shows come together, I had a great deal of help getting Bogart and everything else in place for the production of *Heart of the Sanibel Sunset Detective*.

My wife, Kathy Lenhoff, again played the indispensable role of First Reader and Irresistible Love Interest, transforming our life together into a wonderful romantic adventure, complete with happy endings.

Editors David Kendall and Ray Bennett were excellent as the villains of the piece, making this poor author fix mistakes and plot holes, forcing him to do better. Ray, it should be noted, also does the sidekick part exceedingly well. He was present the night Lauren Bacall tripped over my foot.

Susan Holly on Sanibel Island, our resident heroine, swept in at the end of the show and discovered all sorts of shortcomings that the rest of us had managed to miss. Ric Base, aka my brother, put the production together, kept it on track, and left me asking the question I ask myself each time we work together: What would I ever do without him?

Finally, a salute to our scenic designer, Jennifer Smith, for exercising her creative talents in dressing the overall look of the production.

As for me, by the time one of these books is completed, I feel very much like the novice bit player, thankful to be in the hands of such a smart, professional ensemble cast.

Bravo, everyone!

About the Author

Over his long career, Ron Base has written for newspapers and magazines, including the *Chicago Tribune*, the *Los Angeles Times*, the *Washington Post*, and *Cosmopolitan* magazine. For a decade he wrote about movies for the *Toronto Star*, Canada's largest newspaper. He has also written screenplays, nonfiction books, and novels. He's lived in Toronto, Los Angeles, Paris, Rome, and Montreal. Ron and his wife, Kathy Lenhoff, divide their time between Milton, Ontario, and Fort Myers, Florida, not far from Sanibel Island where his bestselling Tree Callister mysteries are set.

Sanibel Sunset Detective Website
ronbase.com

Contact Ron at
ronbase@ronbase.com

Ron's blog at
ronbase.wordpress.com

COMING SOON

THE DAME

With The Sanibel Sunset Detective